DARK

CURSE

DARK CURSE

DARKHAVEN SAGA: BOOK FIVE

DANIELLE ROSE

WATERHOUSE PRESS

For Nicki—
If you made it this far in the series,
you should stop telling people you're "not a reader."

ONE

I thought the vampire was dead. After the witches dabbled with the black arts, I assumed my punishment for all my misdeeds and bad choices was to live a life just barely grasping the power that lies beyond my fingertips.

It turns out I was wrong.

The vampire has always been inside me. She is now, but we are disconnected, and I have only myself to blame.

Now that I know she is simply slumbering, I feel her. I sense her desires. When she has a particularly restless night, I crave the sweet aroma of blood on my lips and I yearn for vengeance against those who cursed me to live as neither witch nor vampire.

Before, when I only had to worry about *Mamá*'s spell, I was still a witch, but now I am not even sure if I am human. Because of my choices, I am cursed to remain in darkness without the ability to truly appreciate the shadows.

My exile feels permanent, as if I am forever condemned to the void that is nestled within my very soul. I should feel happy here, because I know the vampire is trapped with me. But I do not. Lifeless and still, I remain within the abyss, just waiting for the moment the witches come for me. Because I know they will. The spell I cast was nothing like the black magic they used against me. Hexes can be broken, and therein lies the irony.

I damned myself.

When I cast that spell, the link Mamá formed between us ensured I doomed myself as well. I knew what I was doing. I used the power of both my coven and the moon, harnessing enough energy from the vampire to formally take a stand against the witches. When I used our link to suppress their magic, I suppressed mine as well.

But even though I know I am to blame for the cost I must now bear, my situation never gets easier. I never become less of a burden to those I now consider family.

For one month, I have lived with the vampires as a mortal, but I do not fear for my life the way I do when the witches are near. In fact, the vampires have given me something priceless, something I never experienced under Mamá's roof. Peace.

It has been thirty days and thirty nights since I hexed my former coven, and not a day passes when I do not think about the ramifications of all that has happened since Jasik sired me. He feels responsible. He refuses to listen when I argue that this is not his fault. Over the weeks, I have grown tired of trying to convince him, so now we live in an uncomfortable silence.

I roll over in bed, repositioning my pillow as quietly as I can, desperately trying not to wake the slumbering vampire beside me. If I were still a hybrid, I could have leaped from this bed and run down the stairs without ever making a sound. Unfortunately, the spell that I cast severed my connection to my magical side also suppressed my fantastical abilities.

So I ask myself, what is left when I am no longer a witch or a vampire?

A clumsy human.

Something I have never been but now must embrace.

I open my eyes, letting my senses adjust to the unlit room.

Even though my sense of sight is no longer heightened, if I wait long enough, I can make out Jasik's features. Tonight, it does not take as long as it normally does for me to see him clearly.

He is lying beside me. I shimmy closer to him, desperate for warmth I know I will not find in the body of a vampire. Deep down, I know the chill nestled in my bones is *because* I am sleeping beside the undead, but in my heart, I cannot force him away. I feel safe when Jasik is near.

I poke my head up, peering into my dark bedroom. I do not know the hour, but I know it is daytime. Thick burgundy curtains block out the sunlight except for one solid line at the corner of the window. The sun splashes into the room, illuminating what should be a pitch-black space.

Cursing inwardly, I gnaw on my lower lip. Soon, the sun will make way for the moon, and the chance it will harm Jasik is unlikely. Still, I feel compelled to draw the curtains even tighter.

An invisible force pulls me to the window, summoning me to its side, and all I can do is obey its silent order.

I pull back the covers and rise from bed before I even make the decision to stand. I tiptoe, walking around the four-post bed, trailing my fingertips along the mattress top. My fingers snag in the blankets, and I freeze, glancing over at Jasik.

We decided he would stay in my room the night I returned home. For the first week, he slept in a chair. The next week, I woke to find him on the floor. He balled his jacket into a makeshift pillow. After that, I told him to come to bed with me. He was hesitant, but he conceded when I starting having the nightmares. After several nights in a row of waking the entire manor with my screams, we knew we needed to try something else.

The first night I dreamed, the other hunters—Malik, Hikari, and Jeremiah—rushed into my room, expecting to find a bloodbath, only to see me drenched in sweat, cradled in Jasik's arms as I screamed about the witches and how they were coming for their revenge. The details are still fuzzy. I do not remember most of the nightmares, but I do remember the way they made me feel. That fear has clung to me since the day I escaped captivity, and it is tightening so ruthlessly around my chest, I can barely breathe even when I am awake.

I feel it now. The familiar sense of being asleep leaves a stagnant odor in the air, but still, I have to ask myself.

Am I dreaming?

I cannot always tell. I feel controlled, as if I am not aware of my actions until after I commit them. But this does not feel like a dream. This does not even feel like a nightmare. It is just me and Jasik and the horror my life has become.

He seems unbothered by the rustling of sheets, even though I have pulled them tighter over his frame. I am surprised he is using them at all. He rarely sleeps with the covers on. Too often, I wake to find them bunched all around me, but today, he is covered from his waist down. Still, one leg dangles free.

I am still staring at him when I step on a loose floorboard. I hold my breath. I freeze, letting the room settle into silence once again before I continue—this time actually watching where I am walking.

At the end of the bed, I grip the footboard, my heart steadily hammering in my chest. The constant thump has reached my ears, and it is all I can hear. I try to breathe slowly, calmly, chastising myself for being far too emotionally invested in this window. But even as I mentally berate myself in a sad attempt to regain my composure, my fear never lessens.

I do not know why I am so scared. I am not even sure if my concern is for the sunlight, which is slowly creeping closer to my bed, or because I am desperate not to wake Jasik. After disturbing his sleep more times than I care to admit, I worry that he is not resting enough, especially when he still has his daily patrols.

I have already rounded the bed, and I am now on the side Jasik sleeps on. I glance at him, and he still sleeps peacefully. I find myself wondering what he dreams about and if he sees me. I used to dream about him all the time.

"Are we happy?" I whisper mindlessly, but I quickly suck in a sharp breath, scolding myself for being so stupid.

Jasik frowns and shifts in his sleep, but he does not fully wake. I release the breath I was holding and try to calm my nerves.

I want to touch him, but I do not. I know he would wake. So I allow myself to hover above him. Using my hand, I map the sharp edges of his strong body, balancing my arm several inches above his frame. He never moves, and I am certain he does not even know what I am doing here.

My bed is encased in sheer fabric, but it is pulled back now. I have not used it as an enclosure since the night I returned, when I awoke screaming, fearing I was still in captivity. I looked around, and even with Jasik assuring me that I was safe, I felt trapped. I could not escape. Now, the fabric twists around the four posts that nearly reach the ceiling. I have no intention of pulling it free.

When I bring my hand to Jasik's face, I stop. I pull my arm away, afraid I might lose all sense and touch him. Everything about him is perfect—from his devotion to me to his fierce protectiveness. Sometimes, when I am around him, it is almost too hard to look at him. My hands get clammy, my mind fuzzy, and my chest hurts.

Sometimes I catch him looking at me when he thinks I am not aware. It is the way he regards me in those moments. My heart stops, and I want to die.

I am never afraid when I am with him. Even now, as he sleeps, I know I am safe. But that still has not steadied my heart. It races in my chest, hammering so hard against my rib cage I worry it will break free.

Something catches my eye, and I tear my gaze from the vampire beside me. A shadow moves across the strip of light penetrating the room, and I freeze. I do not move again until my chest burns. Only then do I release my breath and take the final steps to the window.

But I do not dare a peek. I refuse to look outside, to see what awaits in the forest that surrounds the manor. With a shaking hand and weak arm, I reach forward. I tuck the curtain around the bend in the windowsill, pulling it tightly so that the sunlight is completely blocked.

Only when I hear his screams do I realize I did not take enough care to enclose my bedroom in darkness.

I blink several times, awakening from my trance. I shield my eyes, the sunlight burning too brightly against my weakened senses.

My bedroom is engulfed in sunlight, and my bed is immersed in flames. Mesmerized by the fire, I am stunned silent, only regaining my control over my voice when it is too late to save him.

From where he lies on my bed, cast aflame in a fiery rage, Jasik bellows, the agony in his voice like a knife to the gut. His pain encompasses me, cocooning me in its clutch, and his screams penetrate straight to my heart. The accusation of his words wraps around me, looping over and over again, and I know I will never be free of it.

I hear nothing else. His scream falls silent, his pain extinguished, and I am showered in ash. But the fire looms, growing brighter by the second as it spreads to the hardwood floor.

The floorboards feel like molten lava against my bare feet. I look at my arms, where Jasik's ashes mix with my sweat. I swirl the mixture together, frowning at the mess I have created.

Someone is banging at my bedroom door. I hear voices, but I do not bother responding. I do not even look their way.

The air is thick with smoke, and I choke on my breath, sucking in sharp gasps as my chest heaves, my body begging for oxygen. My eyelids are heavy, and my limbs are shaking.

But I do not move. Even though I know my senses should be rapid firing, screaming at me to escape, I do not listen to them.

Because all I can hear is Jasik's voice in my head. His cry is like twine, and it threads around me, trapping me in this place, in this time.

Frozen.

Hollow.

Dead.

What have you done?

That evening, as I get ready for another long night of reading stacks of books that can tell me nothing about my condition, I do not look at Jasik. I fear if I do, he will see the guilt etched across my face. It is in the way I look at him, the way I touch him, the way I say his name. I cannot avoid it, and the more time we spend together, the better Jasik becomes at reading my inner thoughts, as if I speak them aloud.

I know I was having another nightmare last night. If I was not, Jasik would be dead right now—killed by my hand. I shiver at the thought, still letting it invade my innermost consciousness. The images lash out at me, and I flinch, allowing my visions to stain my mind in red.

I need to get better at controlling my emotions. The worst part of my transition—from witch to hybrid and hybrid to human—has been my inability to remain calm, lucid in all situations. Every little thing irks me, as though I am some ticking time bomb waiting to burst. And if it does not anger me, it hurts me. There is never an in-between. Either I am mad or sad, but regardless of my emotions, I am slowly drifting into madness.

I try not to agonize over Jasik's fake death, but the fact that my unconscious self unwittingly sacrificed my sire has left heaviness in my soul. And it smothers me. I carry that presence with me, hoping I can veil my inner thoughts as well as I have been hiding the toll a life without magic has had on my mind and body.

Spring is a few short weeks away now, but it is hard to tell based on the color of our surroundings. The world is dusted in snow, but slowly, the morning sun melts everything.

One of the perks of living in Darkhaven is the change of seasons. Winter is cold and snowy. Spring is rainy and warm. Summer is hot and humid. Autumn is colorful and cool. It is no wonder my ancestors settled here. Darkhaven is absolutely an elemental witch's dream. Everywhere I look, there is something nearby to use when invoking the elements. That is, if I still could.

There is a chill in the air—one that only I can feel. The vampires are immune to the hindrance of the elements, whereas I now wither in them. Everything is either too hot or too cold, too wet or too dry. I am never at peace—not with the icy air blowing over Darkhaven, not with the silent moon, not with the rays of sunshine I attempt to soak up with Holland, not with my decision to oust myself from the magical kingdom I was born into.

I did what I had to do, but is the cost too much to bear?

I tug on the hem of my sweater. I must do this often, mindlessly so, because threads are beginning to come loose where my fingers pick at the fabric. I gnaw on my lip, thinking about my wardrobe.

When I was a hybrid, I did not have to worry about exposure to the elements. Now, that is all I think about—and not just from the elements. My skin. I worry my secrets will not remain hidden for long.

When the weather warms, I will not be able to hide behind the many layers of clothing covering me now. I blame being bundled up all the time on the frosty air, and the vampires believe me, even when Holland lounges in a thin T-shirt. The vampires trust me, believing, after everything we have been through, I would not hide anything from them.

But I do.

Not out of fear or shame. I just...do. I cannot help it. Whenever I think about admitting the severity of my situation, something stops me. I do not know what it is, but it is always with me, waiting, lurking, watching as I succumb to the silence. I have never before felt as lonely as I feel now.

I do not tell Jasik or Holland how loud the darkness has become. I do not admit to my nightmares, even when I wake screaming and Jasik has to hold me close in order to steady my overworked heart. I do not tell him what happens in my dreams, even though I can see the fear in his eyes when he wakes me. He knows something is amiss. He knows my nightmares are becoming far too real for me. Still, I do not admit how close I am to the edge of the abyss, even when Jasik whispers into my ear that he will always keep me safe.

One night, when Jasik thought I was sleeping, he told me he would sacrifice his own life if that is what it took to keep me safe. I believed him. He has always been loyal and honorable in that way. Nightly, he risks death to protect the manor, so I have no doubt he will offer everything he has to save me, for I am his first. I am the only one he offered immortality to, and as I am sired to him, I did not have the courage to tell him it will come to that. Soon, the darkness in me will take control, and it will be him or me. I just hope he makes the right choice, for evil can wear the mask of a girl.

I stare at my reflection in the bathroom mirror. I do not look the same anymore. My irises are a dirty dark brown, murky and cloudy in color. I am pale, my eyes are sunken, and my skin is taut and dry. My cheekbones are more pronounced, and I feel every rib when I hold myself at night.

I use my fingers to brush my hair, attempting to calm my wild mane, but I only end up looking more haggard, the harsh winter air drying what used to be luscious strands. I frown, giving up as I huff dramatically and take in my appearance one final time.

That is when I notice it.

A sliver of something black is creeping up my neck. I

adjust my sweater, hoping to cover it, but no matter how much I shimmy within the fabric, I cannot. It remains there, poking through, announcing its presence to the world I am desperate to elude. I squint, my vision fuzzy, as I try to better look at the mark.

The fine strands, like silky spider webs splayed across my skin, are making their existence known. I cringe. I have known about them for months, using the advantages of winter to hide beneath layers of cloth. I will not be able to do this in the spring and summer, but part of me thinks that does not matter. I will not make it that long anyway. Not with the hex underway. Not with the madness of Mamá's curse slowly stealing my sanity.

I try to convince myself I must come to terms with my fate. This was the only way I could ensure my coven simply let us be. Together, we live out our final days, sinking deeper and deeper into this wretched void. The curse the witches cast upon themselves the moment they dabbled in the black arts has its hold on us, and each second, it grows stronger as we become weaker.

I tell myself I am not simply giving up. I was the sacrificial lamb in the midst of hungry wolves. This fate is my atonement for all my misdeeds and bad judgments, for all the mistakes I made along the way. If I can die in place of the vampires, well, I figure that is a pretty good way to go. I just wish it didn't take so long. The worst thing about dying is *knowing* I am trudging closer to the edge, and all I can do is *wait* for the fall.

My expression sours, and I chastise myself for thinking like that. Every day I am granted to spend with the vampires is another day to be grateful for. I must remember that.

This does not have to be the end. Holland is certain he and Will are close to discovering a way to sever my magical link to the coven, and if it works, I will be released from the aftereffects of the hex I cast. I try to remain hopeful and optimistic, even when all I want to do is hide under my covers and cry.

I thought the worst part of my situation is my eventual demise, but maybe the disaster is losing myself in these erratic emotions. Just when I was finally getting a handle over them as a hybrid, the vampire was ripped from my very soul. And when she left, the void created in her absence has been nothing but a nightmare.

Sighing, I pull open my vanity drawer a little too aggressively. The many bottles of various makeup products I have accumulated over the weeks since I cast my spell slide forward in unison. They rattle in the drawer and slam against the wooden side. An eruption of glass clanking together tears through the silent room, but nothing breaks. Still, I freeze and wait.

A quick knock on the bathroom door alerts me to his presence.

"Ava? Are you okay?" Jasik asks. I imagine his hand is grasping the knob, wondering if he should enter or wait for my response. Even though I locked the door, I know he can break in if he really wants to. The solid wood is no match for a vampire's strength.

Suddenly, I am damp, and I whisk away the sweat beading at my temple. My voice squeaks when I try to speak, and I curse inwardly. I need to be convincing, or he really will charge inside.

"Yes! Sorry. I just dropped something," I lie.

I wait, listening as the floor creaks. Only when I am certain he has left the doorway do I release the breath I was holding.

I exhale as quietly as I can, but my breath is ragged. If Jasik is still outside the door, he will definitely hear my panic, and he will wonder why I am so nervous.

My heart is hammering in my chest, my vision is hazy, my throat is dry. I am absolutely terrified that Jasik will discover I have been hiding my condition. I do not want him to find out like this. If he needs to know, I want to be the one to tell him. I do not want his discovery of my secrets to be when he slams against the door, breaking it from its hinges, because he fears for my safety—only to discover my once smooth, perfect skin is now smeared with tiny black veins, stretching from my toes all the way to my neck.

Still shaking, I grab a bottle of concealer. I dab some on my neck and smudge the color with my fingertips, badly covering the black lines with a shade of makeup foundation that does not match my now-pale complexion. I exhale sharply as I examine my work. Unsatisfied, I apply more. I do this over and over again, wondering if I have been in the bathroom for an unreasonable amount of time. I worry Jasik might really come barging in to see what is taking so long.

Abandoning my mission, I toss the bottle of useless concealer in the drawer, not caring that it smacks against my other products. It makes a loud noise, and I wince as if it shattered. I live this same routine day after day, still surprised by my lack of satisfaction after I apply my products.

If Jasik enters the bathroom now, he either will not notice my makeup hack job, or he will pretend he does not notice the difference in color between my face and my neck. For weeks, I have been applying concealer to any skin I worry might be exposed—from my neck and chest to my hands and arms, and at some point, I am sure he has noticed my newfound interest in cosmetics, especially since I rarely wore makeup before.

I examine my neck. I want so badly to keep applying more concealer until I am bathed in the liquid, but I do not. It does not matter how much I cake on my skin, the faint discoloration from the black veins is still there, subtle but true. If I notice them, Jasik must be able to. Yet he never says anything, and I never catch him peering at me peculiarly. I am grateful he cares about me enough not to force my admission.

I eye the open drawer, tossing barely used products aside as I search for what I know is not there. This crappy concealer is all I have, because I never leave the manor, not even to replace my products or to find shades of makeup that actually match my color.

The only reason I have as many products as I have is courtesy of Hikari. I confided in her my desire for cosmetics, and she did the best she could to pick up the correct products for my skin type and complexion.

Unfortunately, every day, as the darkness within me feeds on my life force, I lose more of my natural color. Soon, I am certain I will be nothing but a pile of bones encased in a leathery, lifeless, blanched shell. I shiver at the thought.

Deciding against mixing concealer and foundation together to create some makeshift formula that likely will not work anyway, I push the drawer closed and return my gaze to my reflection. I grimace at my work, the sight of me leaving a bad taste in my mouth. The splotch of makeup applied to my neck looks even more noticeable than yesterday. I sigh, wondering if it is even possible to become pastier than I already am. Pretty soon, I will be see-through. Then I will definitely have to reveal my magical afflictions to the vampires.

The floor creaks outside the bathroom door, and I know

Jasik is there, directly outside the door. He always waits for me, and we walk down to breakfast together. Without my heightened senses, I no longer hear the house come alive, and it always feels eerily quiet. Everything about this magicless life feels... lonely.

But I know the vampires are still here, and I trust they will never leave my side. Now, since the sun has set and the moon shines down upon Darkhaven, they awaken. I bet most are already downstairs, devouring mugs of blood while laughing, talking, enjoying the eternity they have been granted on this earth.

I snort when I think about how eternity on this planet once felt smothering, as if too much time were just as bad as not having enough. Now I know that was yet another lie I told myself.

Before, I would look into the future, knowing the vast, endless expanse of time before me is simply waiting for memories, and that feeling is nothing like knowing I have too few days left.

I hide my condition from the vampires. Not because I am afraid they will be angry at my lies or because I am ashamed of the link formed between the witches and me, but because there is no way to explain how it feels to know you should have your whole life ahead of you while waiting for your internal fire to be extinguished by forces utterly out of your control.

I pick at my cuticle, pulling the skin until I bleed. I wince as a surge of pain rushes over me.

When my mother cursed me by linking our souls, she damned my emotions and muted my senses. But my ability to feel pain and fear has never been so sharp.

I dab my tongue against my fingernail, letting the blood

drip into my mouth. When it stops bleeding, I pull down the sleeves of my sweater and slide my thumb through the makeshift holes I cut near the bottom hem.

I started altering my tops by cutting thumb-holes into my long-sleeve T-shirts and sweaters after I thoughtlessly pushed up my sleeves one afternoon while researching my condition with Holland. Luckily, he was invested in the book he was reading and did not notice the veins that have threaded their way through my entire body.

My skin is coated with them now. They are scattered along every curve like tattoos, and they feel just as permanent.

Holland never knew he was one blink away from realizing how desperate my situation has become. And just like with Jasik, I do not want him to know. I am dooming myself to mourn my life in silence, accepting my fate as one of the few things I chose.

Terrified Holland might find out the truth because I carelessly pushed up my sleeves, I cut up my clothes, ensuring to never again make that mistake.

TWO

I stare at him just over the top of the leather-bound book I have been thumbing through for the last hour—to no avail. Lately, I do not have the luxury of reading for pleasure. Instead, I am doomed to skim these musty pages until something sticks out as a feasible option.

Streams of words formed by some archaic language no one speaks anymore loop endlessly in my mind, and I wonder if I have been wrong all this time. Maybe *this*—the inability to comprehend my terminal fate—is hell.

In these moments, when the darkness is heavy on my heart, and it is so loud, doubt becomes all I can hear, I like to believe that death offers peace life can never grant me. That thought crosses my mind now, and something settles over me. It feels...weighty and formidable, embracing me until I submit to it.

I shake away those dark thoughts, that ominous feeling. Every day, I struggle to remain hopeful and optimistic that Holland is both smart enough and strong enough to fix me. I am constantly combating my desire to accept my fate and my need to fight it.

In these times of severe doubt, when I just want to give up and enjoy what little time I have left, I forget who I am. I must never forget that I am a fighter. I am a warrior. I am strong enough to withstand any fate, even one brought on by my doing. Sometimes, I bring myself back to reality, but other times, my words are not enough to keep me sane, happy. It is a daily struggle, a constant teeter of emotional whiplash. And I am getting tired of it.

I watch as Holland makes his way through piles of research books long before I finish even one. I wonder if he knows he is trying harder than me. Can he tell I am slowly losing hope? Is it obvious to everyone in this house?

Holland scrunches his face at something he is reading, and I squint, trying to see him more clearly. Ever since I cast the spell, damning my body to live out a mortal life, my vision has worsened. Not only do I not have heightened senses, but I barely have basic vision at this point.

I do not understand how some people open their eyes and simply cannot see. Requiring contact lenses or glasses just to notice your surroundings is a form of cruel and unusual punishment.

Holland groans, mumbling under his breath. He twists in his seat and scribbles something on the notepad beside him. He presses too hard, and the pencil tip snaps. He curses and throws his writing utensil on the floor. It smacks against the hardwood, bouncing several times before it slides to a stop at the other side of the room. It seems my situation is taking a toll on everyone.

Holland peers at me, his brown eyes wide, as if he is embarrassed I witnessed his breakdown. I smile, hoping it seems genuine and speaks volumes to our situation. I want to pull him into a hug and tell him it is okay. We all have these moments. If only he knew how emotionally unstable I am right now, he would not feel so awkward. He would laugh it off, pick up his broken pencil, and start over. I envy him in this moment. My situation is not as easily remedied.

Holland's lids are heavy. Dark circles under his eyes are overemphasized by his pale skin. He apologizes for his outburst and runs a hand through his already-sloppy hair. His fingers get tangled in the mess, so he leaves it in a heap atop his head and drops his arm to his side. He thumbs the edge of the sofa awkwardly, peering up to meet my gaze.

I smile at him, conveying with my eyes that it is okay. I wish he did not take this so seriously. Sure, I want to find a way to sever this link as much as he does, but I hate that Holland is sacrificing his own health to save me.

Everyone is surrendering their lives and their time to this cause—except for me. I am deemed too weak to assist. So I just sit here with my books and my doubt, sinking further into the quicksand, the barren abyss my world has become. As they walk around me, frantically trying to find a magical situation to break a curse gone wrong, no one even notices that I am disappearing.

Soon, I fear I will be rooted so deeply, with the sand all around, I will not be able to breathe. I worry no one will see, no one will notice. I will just be . . . gone. And they will still be searching for a cure.

I continue to smile at Holland, and he returns the gesture, laughing off his tantrum all while these thoughts rush through my mind. My mouth mute, my tongue a useless husk, Holland never notices.

And I sink a little deeper.

Breaking my gaze, Holland snaps the book shut, and a plume of dust erupts in the air. He does not seem to notice that either. He tosses the tome on the open seat beside him and walks across the room to pick up the pencil. After wiping it off, he returns to the couch, never meeting my gaze.

He rarely looks at me now. Only when he needs certain information will he give me his full attention. I think he fears he will not discover a cure, a way to cut the link once and for all, and he does not want me to see that realization in his eyes. So he never meets mine anymore.

Ever since I returned home, the vampires have acted different. They worry. I catch them staring when they think I do not notice, and I try not to let it bother me. But it does. They all look at me the same way—like I am a victim.

And I guess I am now. This is a role I have never played, and to be honest, I hate it. I hate that I am no longer comfortable in my own skin. I hate that I must rely on everyone else just to survive the night. I cannot leave the manor, because danger lurks around every corner in Darkhaven, from covens of witches who hate me enough to damn themselves to rogue vampires intent on annihilating the entire population. Even tripping over my own feet can end in disaster.

I sigh and scan the book I am reading. The words begin to blur together, the ink seeping from the pages and dripping into a pool in my lap. I look away, once again setting my sights on the scene before me rather than the pages that might save me. My mind is too mushy to focus right now anyway.

I hear everything now. The vampires whisper about my condition, only silencing when they hear my approach. The hunters are better at hiding their concern for my well-being. They pretend nothing has happened, even allowing me to sit in on their meetings to schedule patrols. Each eagerly volunteers for every shift, never allowing a vacant night to go by. It's not like I could actually sign up for a slot, but still,

I appreciate that we all pretend I could.

Amicia is the only one who does not play games with me. She makes her concern for my condition clear. Daily, she asks me how I am feeling, if I notice any changes, if I seem to be better or worse. She asks me about the darkness, and sometimes, I think she knows I lie to her. But she never questions me further. I know she accepts me as a member of her nest, but her real concern is for her vampires, the ones she sired, the ones she vowed to protect.

Amicia might not have witnessed firsthand the evil that resides within me courtesy of the black magic used to link my soul to the witches, but she is wise even beyond her many, *many* years. She knows it is only a matter of time before the darkness eats away at my sanity, making me a danger to her and every vampire in this nest. That is the moment she will no longer tolerate my lies.

I frown and play with a loose string at my wrist. The thumbhole I cut into this sweater is already unraveling. The threads that once kept this shirt formed are falling away. I will probably only get another night out of it before I will be forced to toss it in the garbage. I cannot risk it unraveling in front of the vampires. They cannot discover the truth by mere accident, so I only wear clothes a handful of times before asking Hikari to find me more.

I think she is getting suspicious. After all, how many clothes does one girl need? Still, she remains silent, agreeing to find me anything I need. I am eternally grateful to her. I could not keep up my ruse without her aid.

Closing my eyes, I lean back in my chair and inhale deeply. A sharp stabbing pain is becoming more prominent deep within my skull. I finger my temples, applying enough pressure to give me something else to focus on but not enough to make the throbbing inside my head actually fade away. Sudden migraines are swift and daily now. I suppose this is just another perk of being cursed by black magic.

The book I was failing to comprehend is resting on my lap, and it slips, sliding down my narrow legs and landing in a loud heap on the floor. When I open my eyes, Holland is staring at me. He is frowning, not bothering to hide his concern.

Expressionless and guarded, he wears a mask when he is around me, and he uses it to hide his emotions. Every day, I fight the urge to ask him if it is exhausting being hyperaware every single day, never wanting to show too much. But I already know the answer, because I too am wearing a mask. I know just how tiring it can be.

Holland eyes the book now splayed on the floor by my feet and then glances back up at me. I drop my arms, suddenly self-conscious for trying to ease my headache tension.

"Everything okay?" Holland asks.

His eyes are dark, almost black, and I swallow hard as I look at them. I do not know if his irises are just their natural brown color or if my mind is playing tricks on me, making me see what is not there. The darkness within me likes to do that. It feeds on my insecurities, on my fear. While I waste away, it is living lavishly.

I nod and shrug, trying to play it cool. I do not want him to overreact. Holland tends to cause scenes when he does this. The last thing I need is for a house of vampires to be staring me down, watching me as Holland is now.

"Just a headache," I admit.

Holland smiles, but it never reaches his eyes. I have seen this very look numerous times since I returned to the manor.

It is his fake smile, the one he uses when he wants compliance.

"Why don't we call it a day?" Holland says, as if he would actually stop researching.

He asked me this same question a couple of weeks ago. At that point, I actually believed him. I agreed, welcoming the pause in research, thinking we might do something fun instead. We did not. Holland disappeared into the bedroom he shares with Jeremiah. I found him later huddled on the floor with stacks of books cluttering just about every square inch of that room. Never again did I agree to quit early.

I shake my head. "I am okay."

"How about lunch?" Again, he smiles. This time, it is wider. His face is morphing into a creepy Cheshire cat, and I almost want to say no just to see if he can give me something even wider and more pronounced. Is it possible for him to transform his face into an even more eerie creature? Doubtful.

"I am not hungry, Holland," I say, a little annoyed. "Let's just keep going."

Holland sighs dramatically, not bothering to hide his frustration. I lean over and pick up the book I dropped. The throbbing in my head is still a constant thrum, but I try to ignore it, hoping Holland will see that everything is all right.

When I sit back in my chair, worthless book in hand, Holland has his sight focused on the pages of a thick, leather-bound grimoire. He does not look at me again until it is nearly sunrise.

By the time Holland wants to quit researching for the day, my body aches. We have been sitting in the parlor, curled up with countless research books and grimoires, all written by supposedly powerful witches, for half a day's time. And I am starving, my muscles stiff, my eyes heavy. My weak, mortal body was not made for this mental—and somewhat physical—torture.

I stare at the ceiling, noticing the faded paint and chipped drywall, blemishes on an otherwise smooth surface. In the corner, where the crown molding meets one of the walls, the wallpaper is peeling. I have never seen the room from this angle, but I admire the manor's imperfections. It does not try to hide its impurities the way I do. I wish I could lean on it, using its support and strength to amplify my own.

I cross my legs at my ankles and wince as the pain in my lower back shoots down my spine. My body is tight, and I desperately need to stretch.

Rolling my head against the hardwood, I look over at Holland, who is still perched on the couch. I, on the other hand, dropped from the chair to lie on the floor. At the time, I thought it would be more comfortable. I was wrong.

"Need help getting up?" Holland asks.

I want to laugh because I think he is joking. I want to believe he is messing with me. I want to throw my book at his foot or smack his shoulder or roll my eyes. *Of course* I do not need help. I am not an elder!

But I do none of those things. Because I know he is not joking. Holland means what he says, and he truly believes I might need help pushing my weakened body off the floor. Ignoring his request, I turn away from him, letting my gaze settle on the imperfect ceiling once again.

I linger on the fireplace, which, positioned at the center of the room, is a true focal point. It draws the eyes of everyone who enters. But as soon as any visitor steps inside to admire the architecture of the custom piece built specifically for this vampire Victorian manor, their gaze travels the rows of bookshelves stocked with first-edition novels.

Even more are in piles on the floor. From classics to grimoires and historical references, the stacks tower over me, encasing me between seemingly endless rows of dusty, musty pages. None of which has contained even a single helpful word. I am beginning to think the answer is not here.

The smell of something absolutely divine reaches my nose, and I close my eyes, inhaling slowly, deeply, relishing every second of this moment. Because soon it will be gone. With my senses dulled since I was cursed, I am rarely offered moments of indulgence. I lick my lips, my mouth salivating as if I have not eaten in days.

"Come on now," Holland says. "Up we go."

I open my eyes. He is standing over me, his arm outstretched as he offers me his hand. Begrudgingly, I accept his offer, and he pulls me to my feet. I stumble, grabbing on to him to steady myself as blood rushes to my brain.

I blink several times, clearing my vision. Almost as soon as my dizzy spell hits, it dissipates, leaving me with nothing but a concerned-looking witch staring down at me. I find myself wondering what happened to Holland's mask.

His forehead is creased, his eyes narrowed as he squints while he looks at me. Except, he isn't looking in my eyes. Mentally, I try to follow his gaze, to see what has captured his attention so acutely. He stands stiff, his muscles frozen in time as he assesses me.

Suddenly I know what he sees, and I suck in a sharp breath at the realization. Holland's gaze flashes to mine, and a moment of recognition crosses between us. I swallow the knot that forms in my throat and yank myself free of his embrace.

I stumble backward, desperate to put as much space between the two of us as I possibly can. I am willing to put the entire forest between us if that is what I have to do to keep him silent. I do not want to listen to his questions or hear his accusations. I just want silence, even for only a moment longer.

I see it in his eyes. The endless questions that play through his mind, the hurt on his face for realizing my secret, the fear that inevitably consumes him as he recognizes that I have far less time than he originally thought.

"Ava . . ." Holland whispers.

He does not hide his pain. It coats his words, wrapping around me until it chokes the life from me. Holland's agony over my fate suffocates me, and I realize *this* is why I keep my secrets. Yes, I am scared to admit my fate, but more importantly, I do not want to witness these moments. I do not want to see it flash before Jasik's eyes as he understands he must bury the first vampire he sired.

I am going to die—it is just a matter of time.

Holland takes a step forward, but I hold out my arms, stopping him in his tracks. Tears burn behind my eyes, but I cannot let them fall. If I weep now, every vampire in this manor will rush to my side. And I cannot stare down an entire nest while still maintaining my secrecy. I will break. *They* will force the truth from my numb tongue, and I am not ready for that. Not yet. Maybe not ever.

"Please don't," I say, begging for silence but receiving none.

"How long?" Holland asks. He is not specific. I suppose he does not need to be. We both know I understand his question.

I do not respond, but not because I do not want to. My mouth has run dry, my tongue painful to move. Suddenly scorching, my skin is moist, and I dab at my forehead with my sweater. My breathing becomes loud and erratic, my heart pounding in my chest. I feel light-headed as my vision blurs, and I worry I might actually pass out.

Holland wants me to admit my lies, to come to terms with my secrecy once and for all, but the thought of doing so nauseates me. I feel weaker than I have ever felt in my entire life, and I once took a dagger to the back courtesy of my own grandmother. But this is far worse.

"Soup's on!" Jasik shouts as he enters the parlor.

His mouth is upturned in a beautiful smile that is wide and white. His fangs hang down low, betraying his identity as an immortal creature of the night. I notice them every time he looks at me, because mine are no longer there. There was once a time when I hated what I had become, and now, I would give anything to look at myself in the mirror and not hate what I see.

Jasik's dark-brown hair is shiny and silky, his skin pale, his eyes piercing crimson red. His body is toned and tall—much taller than me—yet as he makes his way into the parlor, dressed in his typical hunting gear for tonight's patrol, I go weak in the knees. This dark, dangerous predator walks confidently toward me, carrying a pot of sloshing liquid.

Strapped to his torso is a bright pink apron that says *Kiss the Chef* in bold, black letters that sparkle. Hikari brought it home one day as a surprise for me. She included some cookbooks and said she stocked the kitchen with basics.

"You got this for me?" I had asked her in disbelief when she gave it to me. I had only asked her for makeup and clothes.

She snorted. "Do not act so surprised. You are basically confined to the manor. I thought you might like new ways to spend your time. I mean, what else are you going to do around here? A person could go crazy being locked in!"

She was right. I was losing my mind—though for other reasons—but I did need to find new hobbies, and cooking was a great place to start. Unfortunately, everyone else claimed the space, and I never made it into those cookbooks.

The moment Jasik realizes something is wrong, he halts. The pot of soup slips from his hand. Chunks of meat, potatoes, and vegetables scatter across the floor, the liquid dousing a pile of nearby books. They were probably priceless, but he does not care. He pays no attention to them, focusing solely on me.

Jasik shuffles his way through the room, crushing chunks of food and kicking the useless bound paper to the side as he makes his way to me.

"What is it? What happened?" His eyes are dark, and the concern within them makes my heart sink.

Holland says something, but I do not hear him. My attention is solely on my sire. He reaches my side in seconds, and he wraps his long fingers around my thinning arms. He holds me like this, not too close and not too far, assessing every inch of me. His gaze never lands on my neck, where my mark and horrific makeup job betrayed my secrets only moments ago.

I shake my head, losing my grip over one of the many tears threatening to spill, and it drips down to my chin. I fall against him. He wraps his arms around me, holding me tightly, and I feel like nothing can penetrate his arms of steel. Jasik is strong enough to keep me safe from any physical danger, but when I look up at him, our lips nearly grazing as he looks down at me, I see it.

In his eyes, there is defeat, because he knows he can protect me from any threat that comes knocking at our door, but he cannot save me from the greatest danger of all: the evil residing within my mortal coil. Every day, he watches as I become weaker, thinner, smaller. Every day, I die a little bit, and he sits beside me, holding my hand as I take my final breaths. I know he will always be there, watching, waiting, unable to stop what fate has already set in motion.

Life should not be this cruel.

Gaining better control over my emotions, I sniffle and push away from Jasik. There is nothing I would like more than to fall into his arms and let the time pass in his safe embrace, but I know I can't do that. I need to remain strong—if only for my own sake—because the truth is soon to be revealed.

"What happened?" Jasik asks as I wipe my eyes and adjust my sweater. I fight the urge to leave it lopsided, where I know it will cover the blotches of mismatched concealer, but I know that will only cause more attention.

I shake my head, ignoring Jasik's question, and I dare a peek at Holland, who stands several feet away, arms crossed, brow furrowed. He is not angry with me, but he is insistent in his desires. He wants me to come clean, to admit the severity of my situation, but I can't. Admitting the truth makes it *real*, and I am not ready for that yet. I do not think the hunters are either.

After several seconds pass, Jasik tosses a glance back at Holland and says, probably more forcefully than intended, "Someone say *something*."

"I think the side effect of the witches' black magic is starting to affect Ava," Holland says bluntly.

I shoot him a look of utter betrayal, but I can't be angry with him. He said what I should have. These were my secrets to bare, and I should have confided the truth in Jasik. After everything we have been through, my sire deserved that.

Jasik frowns. "Is this true?"

He wants to hear it from me, so I mentally prepare myself to speak the truth. I nod, throat clenching. Once again, it is hard to speak. Whenever I think about my situation, I can't see straight. My vision blurs, my mind races, my heart screams in my head. My hands get clammy, my legs grow weak, and everything just *hurts*.

Never have I ever been this terrified.

But I am not worried about the others finding out. I am just *scared*. I am petrified of what lies ahead, and I know every day I wake, I am one step closer to the unknown. Soon, I will rise, but it will not be me. The evil thing that bears my face will walk like me and talk like me and even look like me, but it will not be me. Without my sanity, only madness will remain.

I will be silenced by the darkness, forced to watch as it gains control of this body and my mind. From the sidelines, I will bear witness to the terrible deeds committed by my own hand, even though it will be without my consent. This darkness is an intruder, and it wants nothing more than to find its way inside my very heart, to see what lies there and to find a way to tear it apart.

"Will you show me?" Jasik asks, his voice soft. Everything about him is comforting, from the way he looks at me to the sound of his voice. But these words lash out, striking me down.

I squeeze my eyes shut, pretending I did not hear his request. The thought of letting him see the atrocity my body has become makes me feel ill. A slop of bile works its way into my throat, and this time, I cannot push it down. With my hand over my throat, I run. I escape into the adjoining sitting room, throwing open the door to a half bath positioned directly under the stairs that lead to the second floor. The moment I reach the toilet, I expel everything I can, hoping the darkness inside of me will take the opportunity to leave as well, even though I know that to be a futile dream.

When I am finished, I sit back on my knees, resting my bottom against my heels and my hands on the toilet seat. While heaving, I was squeezing my eyes shut so hard, tears now drip steadily down my cheeks. I pat them away with my sweater and wipe my mouth with the back of my hand.

I hear the door creak behind me, and the heavy footfalls of someone entering the bathroom echoes all around me, but I do not open my eyes. I can't bear to see his face right now. The floor creaks under weight, and I do not have to look to know Jasik is here, watching, waiting.

Finally, after I have summoned the strength to look at him, I open my eyes and suck in a sharp, sour breath. Thankfully, I did not miss the toilet bowl, but the contents inside are enough to make me scream.

And I do. I release everything I have. I am angry that this is my reality, pained that I have become a burden the vampires must protect, and terrified of what will come next.

Because the bile coating the toilet bowl is not only thick and black like sticky tar, but it moves, coming to life as it swirls around the bowl, mixing with the cold water in its depths.

Jasik walks over and crouches beside me. He uses his fingertips to loosen the wet strands of hair that cling to my forehead before tucking them behind my ear. He smiles at me, whispering my name. His love for me reaches his eyes, and I lean against him.

After a long silence, Jasik reaches over me and flushes the toilet. We both watch as the substance I expelled from my body is sucked down the pipes, cast out of the manor with one quick thrust. If only every problem could be alleviated so easily.

We remain silent, unmoving, staring at the now-white toilet bowl, even when the floor creaks again and again as the vampires linger to witness my curse.

THREE

I am standing on the front porch. The manor is dark, the air cold. With each exhalation, I see my breath as lacy puffs of steam that cloud my vision. My nightgown blows in the breeze as a bitter chill works its way up my legs. The wind grabs hold of me, an icy burst that settles deep in my bones.

I know I am not alone.

Staring at the front door, I shiver at the realization. I wrap my arms around myself in my fruitless attempt to soothe my nerves. I rub my bare arms as I peer over my shoulder, terrified of what—or *who*—I might find. At first glance, there is nothing there, but quickly, my vision adjusts, revealing my deepest fears.

The woods surround me. The trees loom overhead, casting shadows that move as the wind blows. The nightmarish creatures that dance among the shadows laugh at my pain and my fear. They know the secrets hidden in the night. They know I am not alone.

I am shaking so viciously I teeter back and forth on my heels. My feet are bare, my toes frozen. My hair is loose around my shoulders, and every time it sways in the breeze, it tickles my skin.

Squinting, I search the forest, desperate to confirm my suspicions, even though that seems like a far worse situation to be in. There is a difference between believing you are not alone and *knowing* you are not alone. That startling truth feels like the tip of a blade that teases a throbbing vein. The difference is life and death.

I see nothing unusual at first, so I tear my vision from the forest and look for the gargoyle. I used to greet him daily with a pat atop his smooth stone head, but I rarely leave the manor now. I think hard, but I do not remember the last time I sat beside him, I cannot even remember the last time I crossed the threshold from the vampires' world into the witches'. I suppose it was the night I returned home, after the bloodshed, after the spell, after the curse that condemned me to this hellish existence.

Once again, I feel eyes on me, a gaze that penetrates deep inside, as if my stalker can see straight into my soul. That thought terrifies me because I am forced to acknowledge the truth. If he can see into my soul, does he recognize the evil that now resides there? Does he know it is not me?

This foreign entity that consumes my life is nothing but an intruder. Even as I internally justify its presence, I know whoever lurks within the shadows does not care. Very few who stalk the night care about those who can walk in the sunshine.

In a rare moment of strength, I take a step forward, allowing my toes to dangle over the edge of the top stair. Facing the woods, my courage dwindles steadily. I pump my hands at my sides, trying to keep away the chill while also reminding myself that I am safe. I am only footsteps away from the vampires inside.

But a thought occurs to me. How did I get here? I do not remember how I got outside or when I left my bed. I am desperate to return to those sheets, where I should be slumbering just like the other vampires.

I consider shouting, yelling for Jasik, but something stops me. A set of irises glow in the darkness. They are bold, striking, and crimson in color. I gasp, stumbling backward, falling against the door. The doorknob jabs me in the back, and my kidneys protest the assault. A throbbing pain shoots through my core, and I wince, sucking in a sharp, cold breath.

I do not turn my back on the monster before me, even when his eyes grow larger as he stalks closer. With my arms behind my back, I twist at the doorknob, but it does not budge. Again, I twist it, almost losing my grip from my too-slick hands. The icy air sends constant shudders down my spine, yet my skin is moist from perspiration, from my fear of becoming food for the very creatures I fear.

It feels like a lifetime has passed since I last encountered a rogue vampire, and now that I am far too weak to even stand tall, I am to face one. I will never survive, not without help, for a powerless witch is no greater threat than a human.

I was beginning to think my reputation preceded me, keeping rogues away from Darkhaven once and for all—and maybe it did. But that was before. That Ava—strong and stubborn, powerful beyond her years—died the very night I cast that spell. Powerless, I am forced to fight a superior predator with nothing but my fingernails, which have been chewed down to stubs.

The rogue vampire is charging forward now, and as he steps out of the shadows and into the moonlight, I can see him more clearly.

Wearing only pants, the skin of his torso is smooth and pale. His hands are dirty, his jeans scuffed. His head is shaved, his face scarred from cuts he must have sustained during the many years before he became a vampire. The faint white lines scattered across his skin are all that betray his age.

His eyes are sunken, his irises burning red. His nose was broken once—again, back during a time when he was not such a monster—and the bone never set properly.

His lips are pale and dry, and his teeth are stained by years of bloodshed. My gaze falls to his fangs. They are long and come to fine points, and as he charges toward me, he exposes them, growling like an animal.

His bare feet slam against the frozen ground, the force radiating through the earth and up my legs. He sinks into the depths, but it never slows his pursuit. The muscles in his legs, though hidden by shreds of fabric, are more than strong enough to tear through the frozen tundra that separates us.

My spine vibrates as he draws closer. My arms shake so viciously, I can barely grasp the handle now.

I am still struggling to open the door, yet frozen by the image before me, as the rogue emerges from the tree line. I scream as he crashes through the wrought-iron fence, not bothering to use the gate door.

Dozens of black metal spears shower down, all conveniently missing the rogue. He effortlessly glides around them, unconcerned that one might pierce his chest, penetrating his sternum, tearing through his heart.

The creature before me is like no man and no vampire. He is hideous, with darkness practically dripping from his fingertips like streams of blood cascading from a gaping wound. As he charges forward, the darkness encircling him swarms, coming to life, buzzing all around like happy bees. The sound grows louder the closer the rogue becomes, and it muffles my shrieks.

I turn my back to the rogue vampire, frantically trying to open the door, to escape inside the manor, where I have stupidly convinced myself he cannot go—if only vampires truly did require an invitation to enter.

The door is locked, and no matter how hard I grip the handle and twist or how much I shake it in my hand, it never gives way to my request.

Desperate for entrance, I ball my hand into a fist and slam it against the dark wood door again and again. Surely, the vampires must hear me. From my screams to the constant banging, *something* must wake them.

I slam my fist against the door again, and my wrist screams for me to stop. But I ignore it. I cannot stop. Each second that passes is one second closer to an encounter I am determined to avoid.

I freeze when I hear his footfalls. I do not need to face him to know he is only feet behind me now.

I am screaming inside, my gut begging me to get inside. Sanctuary and protection are just a step away, but I cannot seem to get there.

Suddenly, the air stills. The night silences. I am breathing loudly, and that sound is all I hear. Looking down at the doorknob, which I still grasp, my hair falls to the side—by accident or force, I am not sure. I am shaking so violently, the entire door seems to be clattering beneath my grip.

I feel his breath on the back of my neck. He breathes as loudly and as heavily as I do. I understand that he is taking deep, steady inhalations as he consumes my scent—just like a predator does to its prey.

The rogue hums as he exhales after indulging in my scent. When he mumbles his approval, he blows loose strands of my hair even farther to the side, revealing even more of my flesh.

I picture his teeth—all razor-sharp and pointed, more like a demon from a book than a vampire in real life. Something drips onto my skin and slides down my back. I gag at the sticky substances, knowing it is likely drool.

I am crying. Tears steadily drip down my cheeks, soaking my T-shirt. The moment he touches my skin, by wrapping his hands around my arms, I take my balled fist and slam it as hard as I can against the stained-glass window in the front door. The glass shatters, sending colorful shards into the foyer.

From the doorway, where I stand with my assailant still holding on to me, I search the manor, praying to find the vampires inside, but I do not. I can see straight through the foyer all the way to the dining room at the other side. The house is not only silent and still, but it is also empty. The furniture is gone. The walls provide no protection. Not anymore. Not without the vampires inside.

"You are alone," the creature says, seething. I picture him smiling, enjoying my loneliness.

I tremble as I try to maintain my composure. I squeeze my eyes shut, silently reminding myself that this is a dream. This is a nightmare. This creature only exists in my mind. I must remember that I am safe.

The porch creaks as the monster pushes his body against mine. I cower beneath him and suck in a sharp breath as he grips my arms so tightly, I am certain he will break bone. He does not. He releases me, but I still feel his touch, as if he has left his imprint on my body for all to see.

"This is a dream. This is only a dream," I whisper. With my arms dangling at my sides, I scratch my nails against the palms of my hands, trying to force myself to wake. It does not work, but I refuse to give up.

"But I am real," he whispers. His breath is cool against my lobe.

"Just wake up," I whisper, voice quivering, but I soon find my strength. "Wake up!"

He grabs on to me again, and I jerk upright as he digs his fingers into my flesh. I cry out, but he only laughs at my agony.

"I am no dream," he says. "I am your *nightmare.*"

He leans against me, sliding his tongue across the length of my neck. I squirm within his grasp, desperate to free myself, but he is a solid slab of muscle pinning me in place.

"And I am coming for you, *Ava,*" he whispers.

I open my eyes, jolted by the reality that this monster knows my name. No longer outside, I am in my room, tucked safely beneath my sheets. Still, I do not feel safe. My skin crawls. I can still feel his body pressed against mine, his breath against my neck, his tongue . . . I shudder, trying to forget this nightmare ever transpired.

The ceiling fan above my bed is swooshing overhead, sending bursts of air down on me. I sit up, looking around, making sure I truly am alone. The room is dark, and I shiver as the breeze cools my damp skin.

Still feeling uneasy, I yank the covers off me and stand quickly, breathing frantically as I scan the room, certain I am not the only person in my bedroom tonight.

I walk backward, only stopping when I collide with someone else. I scream, spinning around and thrashing feverishly at my assailant. I slam my fists against him, wanting him to feel the same fear and pain he just forced upon me.

"Ava, stop!" Jasik shouts.

He grabs my fists, clutching his hands over my own. Just

his voice is enough to settle my nerves. I blink repeatedly, clearing my vision until his frame fully forms before me.

I am breathing rapidly, my heart racing in my chest. The moment I see him clearly, I fall against him, letting him wrap his arms around me. I once felt safe when Jasik was near, but slowly, I am losing that feeling altogether.

Jasik whispers to me, his breath blowing my hair atop my head as he tells me it will be okay, that I am safe now, that he will never let anything bad happen to me. He promises to always be here, to always be the one to wake me in these moments. Never does he ask me what I dreamed or what I saw, because he knows it was a nightmare. He knows it is never anything good.

By the time I finally settle enough to shake the feeling of utter dread from my soul, my legs hurt from standing for so long. I teeter on my feet, balancing my weight from one foot to the other, trying to ease the pain in both. I do not succeed. Every day, I am reminded of how different I am now, and every day, that dagger sinks a little deeper into my gut.

Jasik pulls back and smiles at me, running his thumb down the curve of my jaw. His hair is messy from sleep, his eyes tired from restless nights of watching over me. His crimson irises glow in the darkness, just like that rogue vampire's, but I never feel uneasy when I am with him. The only vampires that scare me lurk outside of these manor's walls.

His gaze drops down, and Jasik frowns. I squint, trying to see him more clearly in the darkness. His features darken, and a sudden anguish washes over me.

Jasik grabs on to my arm, turning it too quickly, too roughly, and I hiss. Immediately, he realizes his mistake and drops my arm, He looks at me, sorrow in his eyes.

"Is that from your dream?" he asks calmly.

I frown. "Is what from my dream?"

"Your arm, Ava. Look at your arm."

I glance down, seeing nothing in the darkness. As I walk toward the nightstand to turn on the bedside light, I rub my hand over my arm. I do not feel anything, but when I apply pressure, my muscle screams in protest.

I twist the knob on the lamp, illuminating the room, and squeeze my eyes shut at the sudden assault. The moment my senses adjust, I glance down, sucking in a sharp breath as I take in what Jasik noticed even in the darkness.

I hold out both arms, spinning until I face Jasik. His features are pinched into an unreadable slate, but I showcase my fear without shame.

Because on both arms, there are four slender marks that wrap all the way around. I can't see the backs of my arms, but I am certain a single mark stains my skin as well.

The black marks are already turning purple and blue from ruptured blood vessels, forming bruises in the perfect compressions of handprints.

The rogue vampire told me he was real, not a figment of my overactive and cruel imagination, and now, I believe him.

The manor is eerily silent at breakfast. The vampires file in, preparing their own breakfast while I eat what Holland already prepared for us. No one looks at me, not even the hunters. But I do not care. I am too busy wondering how my nightmare manifested itself into a real-life side effect.

I refuse to believe a rogue vampire has the capabilities to

find his way into my dreams. He knew my name, which again might only be the cause of an unrelenting imagination.

I glance at Holland, and he smiles at me as he chomps down a mouthful of eggs. I do not smile back. I keep my mind focused on last night's events, not pointless breakfast chitchat.

I play with the fabric of my turtleneck, running my fingers against my soft skin. I feel the same, even though I know I do not look the same. The black marks are threading higher with each day that passes. I was too tired to attempt a botched makeup job, so I decided against concealer and opted for even more clothes. If the others noticed, they did not comment on my attire.

I push my breakfast around my plate with my fork, never wincing when the metal scrapes against the dish. My senses are too dulled to be bothered by it, but I can tell the vampires do not like it. Even so, I do not stop. I am lost in thought, replaying my nightmare over and over again in my mind until something makes sense.

If he *was* real, who was he? How did he know my name? How did he manage to injure me? Is it possible it was more than just a dream? The witch I used to be chastises me for asking such stupid questions. Spirit witches can visit the astral plane. Thanks to my introduction with Will, I now know other hybrids can enter my dreams unwelcomed.

But I am not a witch anymore.

And that was no hybrid.

Right?

"Everything okay?" Holland asks, breaking my trance.

I freeze, fork still in hand. I drop it, and the metal clanks against the plate loudly, echoing all through the room. The nearby vampires watch me carefully before they continue nuking their mugs of blood. Slowly, they begin to clear out. I do not blame them. I would not want to be around me either.

I collapse into my hands, resting my elbows on the tabletop. Sighing, I shake my head, only succeeding in rubbing my forehead against my palms.

Suddenly, I remember how I scratched my palms in my dream, trying to wake myself from what I assumed was just another bad nightmare.

I pull back, assessing the damage done, finding nothing but pale, dry skin. I stare at the creases, wishing I taught myself to read the lines as a fortune teller does at carnivals. I never tried before because I only had to close my eyes to see the future. I wonder what my future holds now.

"Ava?" Holland says again. He reaches across the table to offer me his hand, but I do not take it.

"I feel like I am losing my mind," I whisper.

"Tell me about the dream," he whispers back.

My gaze darts to his. "Did Jasik tell you?" I am not truly upset that Jasik informed the others of my midday outburst. What else do I expect of him?

Holland nods. "Do not be upset. We all heard your screams. He was cornered into telling us."

I shrug it off. "He would have told you anyway," I say, sounding far more bitter than I mean to.

I know I am being childish, but I can't help it. I am only seventeen. I am *supposed* to act like a child. I am not supposed to be planning my impending funeral. Sometimes, I think the others forget they have far more years on me.

"Ava..." Holland says, chastising me for my behavior without being too harsh.

I inhale deeply, and before I release my breath, I let my

lungs fill until it hurts.

"Tell me about it," Holland asks again.

I stare at my food as I recount the nightmare. Only when I am finished do I peer over at Holland. His forehead is creased, his eyes narrowed. He looks angry, but I have come to understand he is not upset. This is the face he makes when he is lost in thought. He is considering my words carefully, trying to analyze my dream for some hidden meaning that might make sense. He is trying to find a way to make everything okay again, and I worry he will fail.

"What do you think?" I ask, finally breaking the silence.

"I think you are looking pretty rough, Ava," someone says.

I tear my gaze away from Holland to stare at our intruder. The moment I see Will, I am swarmed with emotion. My heart bursts at the sight of him, and I practically hum with excitement.

"Will!"

I shriek as I jump to my feet and push away from the table, my chair skidding against the tile floor. As I rush over to him, I slam my hip into the edge of the table. Pain surges through me, but I ignore it. I hear the distinct clash of something breaking, followed by Holland cursing under his breath, but I ignore those things too. I am focused solely on Will.

I jump into his arms, and he wraps them around me. He lifts me a few inches off the ground, allowing my legs to dangle in front of him. My spine cracks, protesting as he sways back and forth with me limp in his arms like an old rag doll.

"You said you would not be gone long this time," I say. "Liar."

"I know, I know," he responds softly. "I am sorry."

I inhale deeply, finding comfort in Will's scent. Will is the only other hybrid I have ever met, and I have always felt an immediate, innate connection to him. He makes me feel safe and happy and understood. He never cared about my mood swings or blood lust. He understood why I felt so torn between the vampires and witches, and why I fought so hard to protect them, to include them, to end this feud.

He understood because he lost everything at the hands of rogue vampires—just like I did. Our lives collided at the perfect moment, right when I needed him most, and I like to think he was a gift from fate as apology for ending my life so abruptly.

Will chuckles as I bury my face in the crevice of his neck, inhaling deeply. He smells like sage and herbs and spices from spells. He smells like wild flowers and summertime. He smells so familiar, it makes my heart burn. Every time he leaves, I break a little more. I am not sure how many more times he can chip away at me before I shatter completely.

"I missed you too, Ava," Will says.

He squeezes me tightly, and I grunt loudly. My body protests again, but I ignore it. I relish in these moments, because I know, soon, he will leave again. He never stays longer than he must, and it kills me every time I watch him walk away, wondering when—or *if*—he will ever return.

"Careful," someone says.

I open my eyes, finding Jasik a few feet away. He is standing directly behind Will. Something flashes in his eyes, but he blinks, and it is gone. Jasik has never acted jealous of my relationship with Will, but I know it bothers him to see his sire become so invested in another person. Still, I try to be respectful, because even though we have never spoken about it directly, Jasik and I have become something more than *just friends*. We both need each other in ways I have never experienced, and if life would stop spinning out of control for just a minute, I might have the opportunity to find out what it is like to be loved by someone else.

I pull away from Will, and as I take a few steps back, I adjust my shirt to make sure no skin is showing. This has become a mindless routine now. Sometimes, I do not even realize I am doing it. Like now, as Will eyes me curiously, watching as I pull down all the edges of my shirt. My cheeks burn.

"I have missed you," I confide, both in honesty and to distract everyone from witnessing my act.

Will smiles, his dimples piercing his perfectly smooth skin. He was lucky. When Liv died, his link to my coven was severed. For him, it ended with her the moment Hikari killed her. Liv paid the ultimate cost before I was able to hex my coven, so the burden I carry is never on Will. I hold it all, even though he feels responsible for my actions.

Will and I never spoke about that night. He left as soon as I started feeling better, and after that, I never shared my agony over losing Liv with anyone. She might have been molded into the shape of a monster—courtesy of my former coven—but she was once my best friend. We thought we would grow old together.

Looking back, we were crazy to think we would ever grow up. After all, we lived in Darkhaven. We hunted vampires. Nothing about our life was normal. If this place was nothing else, it was a thief of youth.

"Tell me about your travels," I say as I grab on to his hand and pull him back to the breakfast table. I take my seat and keep my gaze on him. I am smiling so widely, my face actually hurts, but I cannot help it. Will brings joy out of me, and I really need happiness right about now.

As I sit, I rest my arms on the table, noticing the broken glass piled atop my plate. When I stood, I must have knocked over my glass of orange juice, because the pile of napkins are stained orange, and my glass is nowhere to be found. I push aside my plate and return my focus to Will, eager to hear about the wonderful places he has been.

"Well, I have some good news," he says, side-eyeing Holland, who immediately freezes. He was lifting another forkful of eggs into his mouth, but now, the utensil is hovering in the air, eggs cooling as he waits for Will to continue. Holland drops his fork and wipes his mouth with his hand.

"What have you learned?" Holland asks, leaning forward. He rests his elbows on the table, while I sink farther into my chair.

I cross my arms over my chest, already annoyed by this turn in the conversation. I was hoping for exciting details about exotic places I will never get to visit. I want to live through Will's adventures and pretend I will one day travel too. The last thing I want to talk about is Will's discovery.

I want to hear about his trip, but only the fun parts. I want to hear how he is *living*. Where has he been? Who has he met? What has he seen? Shortly after I spelled my coven, Will made a pact with Holland to help him find a cure. He left the manor that night with the intention of traveling the world, meeting with powerful covens in an attempt to save me. And he takes his work far too seriously. He never writes, he rarely calls, and when I finally see him, he is all about business.

"I met with some witches who showed me how to sever the link to Ava's mother," Will says.

This catches my attention. "That is not possible," I say. "You cannot reverse the effects of black magic."

I might not be an expert in the black arts, but Holland and I have done more than enough research to know these facts.

Will shakes his head. "You are not understanding. I can sever your connection to the witches by cutting that link. I cannot reverse the black magic. The witches will still suffer those consequences."

"I—but..." I stutter, losing my train of thought as I consider what he is telling me.

"Black magic is a powerful, evil entity, Ava," Holland says. "The witches harnessed it, and someone must pay that cost. But it should not be you."

I swallow, my mouth suddenly dry. I glance at Jasik, who looks happier than I have seen him in weeks. Only moments ago, he looked betrayed, almost jealous of my relationship with Will, but now, that emotion is gone, masked by his outright glee in Will's discovery.

How can everyone be so sure this is serious?

My chest hurts, and my mind is spinning. So many thoughts are swarming in my head. It feels dizzying when I try to settle on just one.

"Ava, this is *good news*," Holland says. He reaches for me, grabbing my hands between his own, but I jerk away. He frowns and sits back, as if I physically lashed him. That is twice now that I have pulled away from him, and though I do not mean to target him, I can't bear to be touched. I need space.

"I—I don't know," I whisper.

"What do you mean?" Will asks.

"Is it a good idea to risk using *more* magic?" I ask. "I mean, we do not even understand the spell they cast to begin with."

"But we can still break it," Will counters.

"What are you afraid of, Ava?" Jasik asks as he crosses his

arms over his chest. He eyes me curiously, trying to read my emotions, which unfortunately, is a lot easier to do now that I am human.

"I just ... I am scared of the consequences," I admit.

"I think the consequences of not even trying are far greater," Will says pointedly.

"Are they?" I ask. "How can you be so sure?"

"Ava, the consequence you are faced with right now is *death*," Holland says. "What can possibly be worse than that?"

I break his gaze, looking down at my hands. I play with a hangnail on my finger, flicking the dead skin with my other fingernail. The vampires do not understand the evil inside me. They see glimpses of it, but they do not truly comprehend what it is or what it is capable of.

The evil inside me moves. It grows stronger as it feeds on my very essence to strengthen itself. It wants to live. It wants to take control of my body and never let me go.

Relinquishing my body to a supreme evil force seems like a far worse fate than death.

FOUR

The house is noisy with vampires. While the others welcome Will's return and celebrate his hopeful news, I sit alone in the solarium.

The large, expansive sun-room wraps around the right side of the manor, from the front parlor, past the adjacent sitting room, and all the way to the dining room at the back of the house. There is a corner doorway to the parlor, which is almost always shut, and two massive double doorways to both the sitting room and dining room.

From where I sit, directly in front of the walkway to the sitting room, I can peer into the other rooms, where groups of vampires are congregating. I never let my gaze settle on one vampire for too long, because I dread the inevitable connection and thumbs-up that will soon follow.

They are happy for me, for the news we just received, and I am grateful to be loved and accepted as a member of a vampire nest meant for Amicia's vampires, not Jasik's. I also appreciate everyone's enthusiasm, but I can't help wondering *why* they care so much. Is it truly because they were fretting over my doom? Or is it because Will brings hope—hope that I might not go insane and murder everyone in their sleep?

I have a feeling the latter rings true for them.

Sure, they are happy for me, but they are still vampires. No one understands the fear of death better than creatures who were supposed to be promised eternal life. Their number-one priority is their own survival, their own safety. My weakening mind and loose grasp over reality poses a great threat to their happy existence. I try not to think about that right now. Instead, I focus on my surroundings, letting the many distractions the manor offers clutter my mind.

I used to be able to sit in this very spot, open both doors, close my eyes, and hear the waves crashing in the distance. I could smell the salty air, feel the tingle of mist against my skin. When I close my eyes now, there is nothing but silence and darkness—much like my future.

I lean back against the wicker sofa I have claimed, pulling my legs up so I can sit cross-legged on the cushion. I teeter, grunting because this simple effort exerts me. When I have finished tucking my feet beneath my legs and finally steady myself so I do not tumble over, I am breathing heavily. If the vampires notice, they do not say anything. I do not look at them either, because I hate what I see when I do.

Pity.

All I ever see anymore is pity, from the hunters and Holland and Amicia and all her vampires. Everyone feels bad that I am slowly dying. Do they not understand that I can't bear spending my final days drowning in my sorrows? I am up to my neck in water, frantically searching for the shallows as I breathe in the murky depths.

If I do not want to talk about it or even think about my situation, I certainly do not want to see the anguish in their eyes.

With my hands in my lap, I scratch at my cuticles, picking until another hangnail bleeds. I wince as blood pools into a tiny bubble. It is so small, barely even a speck of a dot, but the black is so bright against my pale skin. I wait for it to seep into my nail bed, but it does not. There is not even enough blood to fill that tiny line at the base of my fingernail. I think about what I am doing right now and come to a stark realization: maybe I really am pathetic.

"Ava," someone says, and I tear my gaze from my hands, looking up to meet her eyes.

Amicia is standing before me, frowning as her gaze lowers to my hands. I must look pathetic next to her. From where I sit, Amicia looks tall and lanky, and she radiates a powerful essence.

Ever since I cast my spell, I have not felt that innate draw to her that I once did. As a vampire, I could sense her strength even if she was not in the same room as me. It had a smell to it, and the scent lingered in the air. Amicia has a pull, an allure in her aura that makes her formidable. She is probably the oldest, most powerful vampire I will ever meet.

Her black dress looks silky and shimmery as it cascades down her frame. The arms are lacy and pristine. Her hands are collapsed at her waist, her nails painted black. Her hair is shiny and sleek, brushed back and tied tightly behind her.

Jasik approaches us, and I look over at him in time to see his expression change. He is concerned about something—but what? I look back at Amicia, but she is looking over at Jasik now. She shakes her head, waves him away with her hand. Her hair, which is twisted into a bun at the base of her neck, glistens in the light when she moves.

Amicia returns her attention to me, ignoring Jasik until he begrudgingly leaves us. The other vampires back away as well, but I catch sight of them before they go. Their eyes are wide, *hungry*.

I gasp, glancing down at the speckle of blood that is already drying. How could I have been so stupid? I am a *human* in a house full of *vampires*. How ignorant can I be to harm myself in front of them?

"How are you feeling today?" Amicia asks, sounding much more like a therapist than a vampire.

I shrug. "I was not thinking."

She smiles at me. "It is okay."

She ushers to sit down beside me, so I scoot over, dropping my legs to give her space. The soles of my shoes land in a thud against the tile floor.

Amicia sits but turns so she is facing me. She eyes me curiously, not speaking.

I begin to gnaw on my lip, waiting for her to say something, until the silence is so loud, I have to speak.

"I am sorry," I whisper.

"For what?" she asks, seeming thoroughly confused.

"I should not have ... " I glance down at my lap. I wipe the dried blood from my hand, flicking the remains to the floor with one quick thrust. I fist my hands and bury them between my thighs. Maybe if the vampires cannot smell my open wound, they will not feel the desire to rip out my throat.

Amicia pulls my arms free and rests a hand atop my wrists, soothing my nerves with one simple touch.

"I know this is difficult for you, Ava," she says.

I nod, my mind flashing to the last time she and I spoke alone in the solarium. She ended up forming a blood promise with me, which still has not been broken. There are so many strange quirks to magic. These are the moments I realize how similar vampires and witches truly are. Both creatures use blood to form unbreakable bonds.

"I hope you know that I still consider you a member of this family, even if you are no longer a vampire," she continues, and my heart swells.

I smile at her, genuinely, purely, relishing in the familial love she showers over me. Amicia has only known me for a short time, but she has already shown me more support and greater trust than the witches ever have. It is strange that the people we love most are not necessarily sharing our life's blood.

"Will told me about his trip," Amicia says.

I frown, casting my gaze away from hers. But the moment I look down, Amicia's hand catches my chin, bringing my gaze back up to meet hers. She taps the bottom of my chin lightly but firmly, a clear motion in an order to keep my chin up, my head held high.

"Throughout life, we are tested during times when nothing seems fair," Amicia says. "Your choices in these moments reflect your character. I know you are scared. Never in all my years have I met someone quite so—"

"Stubborn?" I interrupt.

"Selfless," Amicia corrects.

"You are a generous soul, Ava," she says. "You give all that you have to everything you do and to everyone you love, even if they are undeserving of such devotion."

I swallow hard, nodding. Amicia has never been fond of my link to the witches, and now it must just kill her to know there is an actual bond formed. Their claws are rooted deep now, and she knows I may never escape.

"Yes, you are rash and impulsive, but your tenacity is impressive. You have an unshakable will to protect those less fortunate than you. You might be reckless and relentless in your pursuits, but you are young. As much as you do not want to hear this, you are still a child. You have so many years ahead of you. Promise me, if you grow up, you will never lose the strong, independent woman you are becoming. Hold on to her, because she will never lead you astray. The warrior within you is worth your admiration and your loyalty. *She* is who you should devote your life to protecting. She is who you should nurture."

"*If*," I whisper, echoing her words, my voice broken. "You said *if* I grow up, not *when*."

Amicia smiles softly, but it does not reach her eyes. "I will not force you to choose. This life is yours, and you should do with it what you want, not what someone else forces you to do. I have made it clear to every vampire in this house, including Jasik, that you are not to be pressured into completing Will's spell. If you wish to sever your link, you have my full support. But if you wish to stay this way, I hope you know how much I have greatly enjoyed getting to know you."

As Amicia speaks to me, it feels as though she is saying goodbye, like she already knows which path I plan to walk. The realization of her words begins to settle over me. I do not want to die, but I am terrified of using even more magic. Every day, the evil within me gets stronger, stealing my life bit by bit. What if I am too far gone now? What if using this spell will be the boost it needs to finally take control? I will lose these last few weeks of sanity in one moment of empty promises.

"Enjoy yourself today, Ava. Do not worry about curses or magic. Just have fun. Think about your options, and remember, this is no time to be impetuous. Consider things carefully before you make your decision. Either choice comes with a cost. You must be prepared to bear that weight regardless of how you plan to spend your remaining days."

With her final words, Amicia stands and walks away. The moment she crosses the threshold into the sitting room, she begins to glance back, but as soon as I see the corner of her eye, she stops. Maybe she whispers something, maybe she does not. My senses are too dulled to know for sure. She continues walking away, more hastily now, until she disappears among the vampires.

"She is pretty intense," Will says as he walks over to me. He glances back, gaze trailing the path Amicia cleared as she left the room. The other vampires part for her without hesitation or request. I wonder what it feels like to have such a devoted following.

"A little," I admit.

"Can I join you?" Will says. He tips his head at the vacant seat, now even cooler after Amicia left.

I nod, and Will sits down beside me. He settles in a huff, dramatically stretching out as if this were the first time he has taken a break in days. For all I know, it has been. He still has yet to provide details regarding his travels.

"Are you ever going to tell me about your trip?" I ask, not bothering to hide my annoyance.

"We did talk about it," Will says. He glances over at me and chuckles as I roll my eyes. "You want to know about the fun stuff."

It is not a question, so I do not respond. We sit in silence, both watching the vampires mingle. It almost feels like a party, but I am not sure even they know what they are celebrating. Normally, the vampires of the house keep their distances from the hunters. I am not sure if this is by choice or by order. I suppose no one wants to get too close to someone who is one bad battlefield move away from death.

"It is strange, isn't it?" Will asks.

I blink away my thoughts, following his gaze. Several feet in front of us, I watch as Holland and Jeremiah laugh at something inaudible. Holland leans against Jeremiah, and the vampire opens for him, holding him closely. When he thinks no one is looking, Jeremiah softly kisses Holland's forehead and runs his fingers through his hair. He says something, and they both laugh. My heart burns as I watch them. While I am happy for their reunion, I can't help my jealousy.

I frown, looking at my friends more closely. "What is strange?"

"The last time I was here, they were not exactly on friendly terms, were they? I could tell something was there—the ice was beginning to thaw. But isn't it strange how one day, one thought, one action can decisively change your life?"

"How so?" I ask, still unsure of what Will means. I can tell he is on the brink of forcing an epiphany. Usually I am not interested in his wise ways, but today is different. Seeing my friends celebrate my life, especially when I am not sure I even have good news to share, only makes me feel like I am slipping further away from everything I once knew.

"I know they used to be in a relationship," Will says. "That was always obvious by the way they would argue. They were snippy, personally so. The way exes are."

"And?" I ask, suddenly intrigued by where this might be going.

"And now look at them. They act like they haven't been feuding for, what, the past several years?"

"I suppose death brings that out in people," I say, finally understanding where Will might be taking this conversation.

Death changes you. When people find out they do not

have many days left, they act differently. They love harder, they forgive easier, and they are kind to strangers. When onlookers witness death firsthand, it affects them too, even if they are not the one slipping away. Watching as I grow sicker by the day is affecting the vampires. I am just grateful one positive thing has come out of my sacrifice.

"Death has nothing to do with this, Ava," Will counters. "*You* brought this out of them."

"I guess I did."

Will nods. "They looked at your situation and realized how precious life is, how they have been wasting the days they were granted by prolonging the inevitable—reuniting."

"Are you saying I am wasting my life?" I ask, crossing my arms over my chest.

"I think you are, yes," Will says plainly.

"Or maybe I am taking a bullet for the team," I counter.

"We are *immortal*, Ava. Let us take that bullet for you."

When Will looks at me, his eyes are heavy. I know he is tired from his travels, but the emotion there is true—and it is for me. Will feels the very same connection that I feel when he is around. It is complicated but true.

I wonder if he has ever felt this way before. Am I the first hybrid he has ever met? Everything happened so quickly after he found me. I never had the opportunity to ask him about his life before the witches went and messed up everything.

"I know you are scared," Will says. "And I promised Amicia I would not push you, but—"

"But you are a liar?" I say, grinning.

"She asks a lot from me," Will says, "but she must know by now that my loyalty is not to her."

Will meets my gaze, and we sit in silence for a long time as his words settle over me. I swallow hard.

"I hope you know I am loyal to you too," I whisper.

"I know you are—stubbornly and annoyingly so. You will not even let me take the fall for this one when I am clearly better suited for this burden."

I roll my eyes and look back at the party. Jeremiah is holding Holland now, and they both sway side to side to music no one hears but them. I smile, hoping if I stare long enough, I can burn the image of them into my brain. I want to see them this happy for the rest of the time I have here.

"I will not force you to complete the reversal spell, because it is only right that you make the choice for yourself. But I think you are an idiot for not even trying."

I snort. "Thanks."

"I know you are confused, so let me say just this last bit. Then I will never bring it up again. I know you are scared because we have to dabble in dark magic to sever your link. I know that worries you, and I know that is the only reason you will not try. Before you make an impulsive decision based on fear alone, stop. Think. You need to figure out who you are, who you want to be. That is when you will know if you should sever this link or bear the consequences."

"I am just not sure if it is worth the risk," I admit.

"*You* are worth it, Ava. You are worth every risk. Do not ever forget that."

After a few silent minutes pass, I am thoroughly tired of talking about the spell, but I know he will not let me off so easily. I remember Will's earlier emotions, so I decide to turn the tables on him.

"Why don't you ever talk about your past life?" I ask.

He shrugs, remaining silent. I expected this reaction, but

he has gotten to know me well over the past several weeks. He should know I will not give up this easily.

"You don't think that is actually going to silence me, do you?" I ask.

Will smiles but does not look my way. He keeps his gaze focused on the vampires before us. No one pays us any attention, and I think he likes it that way. I know I do.

"You are headstrong and persistent, so . . . no."

"Tell me *something*," I beg. "Anything at all. Tell me about your life before you became a vampire or your trip just yesterday."

"I became a vampire a long time ago, Ava. Like it is for most, it was not a pleasant experience," Will admits. "I do not care to relive that moment by sharing it now."

"Was it as bad as my transition?" I snort, not expecting a real answer.

"Worse," Will admits quietly.

I narrow my gaze, trying to assess his emotions. He does not look at me, and I have to wonder if he is just trying to silence me.

"How could it have been worse?" I ask.

"You could have lost everyone in that single moment."

I did, I think but remain silent.

"Believe it or not, I understand why you would not want to be a vampire again," Will says. "Sure, we are basically superheroes without the ugly costumes, but we are lonely. Most of us do not have these fancy parties or a nest full of vampires who consider us family. We do not have a home or a sire to love. We are forced to walk this earth without any real family. We live alone, we stick to the shadows, and we try to live out days unseen. Most do not have the luxury of a friend."

Terrified speaking will only make Will realize the personal details he is sharing with me, I swallow the knot in my throat and wait for him to continue. The silence that stretches over us feels endless, and I worry he might never speak about this again. But I can't let him stop here. I have to know more. I have to know *who* Will is. Deep down, he carries a heaviness with him, and it is destroying my heart to know he is in such pain.

"If I were in your situation, I would not want my powers back either. I would live my days as a human, maybe actually meet someone who can relate to me now that I am not constantly craving her blood."

"Then why do you want me to sever the link and reverse my spell?" I ask, confused. The question bursts from me before I realize I am even speaking, and I groan internally, worrying Will might clam up now that I have spoken.

"Because I am selfish and weak. That is all I have ever been."

"You are not weak, Will. You are not even selfish. You single-handedly helped me try to locate Liv when no one else would. You did not know her. You owed her nothing, yet you risked your life to help me locate her. That is not something a selfish person would do."

Will smiles. "You only see the good side of me. You do not see the side that is desperate not to lose you. I finally found someone who understands what it is like to be . . . different. Not human. Not witch. Not vampire. But *something else*. And I am terrified I will lose you, and I will be alone again. I want you to complete the ritual, but that does not mean you *should*. I mean, and I hate to say this because I worry it will influence your decision, but I would not do it if I were you."

I think about what Will says, about how hard that

admission must have been for him. I understand what it feels like to feel so utterly devoted to someone, you would die for him or her. When I think too hard about my feelings for Jasik, that is what I sense. Unrelenting, unstoppable, uncontainable devotion. And it scares me.

"But that is the difference between you and me," Will says. "I do not want this life. I can tell you do. You have all this . . . " He nods at the vampires mingling in the other room. "Look around, Ava. There are dozens of vampires here. All of them would probably die for you. You have a family. You have the one thing I have searched this earth for but failed to find."

"I am sorry," I whisper.

Will frowns. "Why are you sorry? It is not your fault that my life is like this."

"But it is . . . " I say.

"How? You did not bite me. You did not leave me to watch as you murdered my entire coven while I went through the agonizing transition. You did not leave me to wake alone, to come to terms both with my change and the loss of my family in the same horrible minute. Nothing about my pathetic life is your fault."

"The vampire was suppressed," I whisper. "Hikari killed Liv in order to help me, and in doing so, she sacrificed your freedom from darkness. If she did not—"

"If she did not, I would not have been revived. If I was not a hybrid right now, I would not have been able to travel the world, and I would not have discovered the reversal spell that you need to find yourself again."

I shake my head, realizing there is no point in arguing. Will and I will never agree on where to place the blame. I feel responsible for everything that has happened until this point, even if he refuses to see it the way I do.

"Look at me, Ava. I would change nothing, *absolutely nothing*, about the past couple of months. I searched for another hybrid every day since I transitioned, and when I finally found one, I clung on to her. I never had any intention of leaving you behind. I knew the vampires would trust me in time, and I knew you would too. I regret *nothing* about our encounter and the events that occurred after. You should not either."

"I wish things could be different for you," I admit.

"Me too. In all my travels, I have met some pretty powerful witches. I might have found a way to sever that link so you can reverse the spell and restore your powers, but I have not found the key to what I really want."

"And what is that?" I ask.

"A cure."

I frown. "A cure? To vampirism?"

"Well, I would settle for a spell so I can trade places with you."

"You mean you want to sit back and wait as you lose your sanity? Or do you mean you want to walk in my shoes because I am surrounded by all of them?" I ask, glancing at the vampires.

"Both," Will says, chuckling.

"Family can make you crazy," I agree.

We both sit in silence, watching as the vampires flutter about, talking, laughing, indulging in another day that is the most recent in a string of endless days on their timeline. Tomorrow, they will do the same. And the next day. And the next.

They watch me as I waste away, but do they really see me? Do they see how close I am to the edge? Do they know how lucky they are to have the one thing I would kill for?

Time.

I just need more time—time to think, time to plan, time to *live*. I might be ready to take that bullet for them, but that does not mean I would not postpone the inevitable if given the opportunity. If I had the choice to die today or die tomorrow, I would choose tomorrow and spend today with them.

The irony is that I once had the time I now crave. Now, time is fleeting. I think about Will's advice. The clock is ticking, and I need to decide what I want in life.

Do I want to be a vampire again?

Am I strong enough to participate in the ritual and fight off the evil lurking inside me?

I like to think so.

I think I can beat it.

Just as I firmly determine that this evil will never be strong enough to overtake my soul, that I will always come out the winner in this fight for my survival, the evil twisting within my gut springs to life.

And inside me, the darkness laughs.

FIVE

My bedroom is dark and cold. Everything about this house used to invite me in, from the mere sight of it to the way it sounded, the way it smelled. But with each day that passes, I become more disconnected from the creatures who call this place home.

I sit on the edge of the bed, pretending it does not bother me that I left the party early. The gathering downstairs is loud, and voices echo through the halls all the way upstairs. Everyone is celebrating life, cursing death, and welcoming Will into their innermost circle, yet he admits that he feels as lonely as I do right now.

He is cursed to spend an eternity without a partner who truly understands him.

And so am I.

We are so similar, yet so different, so separated from everything we cherish. He yearns for a family, for a place in this world, and even though I have one, even though I have everything he is searching for, I still feel as out of place as he does.

I sigh heavily, allowing myself to sink a little farther into my bed. I am thinner now, and when I look at my skeletal frame in the mirror, I notice prominent arches from bones I have never seen before. I always knew they were there, of course, but my muscles were always hiding these breakable parts of me. Not anymore, even though I am still supposed to be protected by muscle and strength.

Now, knowing how vulnerable I am, I wince when someone moves too quickly around me. I am forever fearing the inevitable assault and snap of bones that are in desperate need of nourishment, even though I eat. A lot. I eat so often, I am actually sick of eating, which is a feeling I never knew existed. But every ounce of food I consume never seems to strengthen my body. It is as though the darkness within me consumes the calories, spitting them out long before I am given the opportunity to indulge as well.

I wrap my arms around myself as a burst of cool air brushes against my skin. I shiver, glancing up. My ceiling fan is forever swirling above me, regardless of how cold it might be outside or inside. Before, I welcomed the different sensations the fan caused. I liked the whooshing sound it made and the tingle of the air against my skin. Now, I only keep it on for the white noise. Every creak, every sniffle, every mumbled breath is a stark reminder of my difference. And I hate it.

A sharp knock against my bedroom door has me jolting upright. I know I have nothing to fear. No one could enter this house and bypass the flock of vampires downstairs without alerting them to an intruder's presence. I am safe here. The vampires will protect me. Still, I cannot calm my racing heart. Every sudden change leaves me with one staggering impulse: run.

I stand so quickly, I become dizzy. Blood rushes to my head, blurring my vision. I wobble, waiting until the feeling subsides. Sometimes it feels like that wave of uneasiness never goes away. It is always there, haunting me, reminding me of how things used to be, of how I will never again walk this earth. Even in times of clarity, that sensation is still there. The only difference is I have gotten used to living with that sickness.

"Come in," I shout as I use the footboard to steady myself. I blink away my blurred vision, trying to focus on my visitor instead of the throbbing in my head.

Jasik enters, one hand grasping the doorknob, the other hiding something behind his back. The moment he sees me, he frowns. His brow furrows, his eyes grow heavy. I hate when he sees me in these moments of weakness, and I imagine he does not care for it either. Every day, he is reminded that I am not the girl he sired so many moons ago.

"I am fine," I say, answering his silent question. I pray he will not push further. I am not in the mood to discuss my feelings. I came to my bedroom for peace, not torture.

I glance down, trying to sneak a peek. I can tell he is hiding something behind him by the way he awkwardly maneuvers through the doorway.

I squint, trying not to think about the fact that I have to squint to see him, even though he is only feet from me. I appreciate times like this, when I have something to focus on other than my doom.

"I have something for you," Jasik says.

I smile widely, suddenly overjoyed. These moments, when I can forget about how the world is slowly crashing down all around me, are the ones I replay over and over again at night, when I am trying to sleep and only want to see the good parts from my life now. I fear closing my eyes, never knowing if I will be offered serenity or a nightmare, and I am hopeful tonight will bring me a cherished memory to loop.

I hold out my arms, pumping my hands into fists over and over again, silently telling Jasik to give me whatever it is. Like a child, I have no patience. I want my present *now*.

"Gimme," I croon, smiling. "Gimme! Gimme!"

My reaction makes him smile, and I take in his appearance as he approaches me. Jasik is tall, leanly built, with boyish charms even though he is centuries older than I am. He died in his early twenties, so he will forever remain in that mid-stage appearance, when he can pass for a kid in his late teens but still might con his way into a bar.

Jasik ushers for me to meet him on the side of the bed, and I quickly prance over. I plop down, letting my legs dangle over the side. I sway side to side, bursting with energy as Jasik slowly approaches me, a sly grin across his face. He is enjoying this moment, taking his time as he strolls to my side.

As he motions to sit down beside me, he tells me to close my eyes. I obey. When I dare a peek, I find him sitting still, silently watching me with his mouth curved into a grin.

"I know you better than you know yourself," Jasik jokes.

Rolling my eyes, I grumble and squeeze my eyes shut tightly so he knows I will not chance a peek again. Still, he makes me wait. The grandfather clock in the hallway ticks loudly, and I find myself swaying to its beat. Only when I feel Jasik place something on my lap do I open my eyes.

A large, rectangular, black box is resting against my lap. Jasik is holding the outer edge so that it remains upright and does not spill onto the floor. I grab on to the edges, prompting him to release it. I feel his gaze on me as I assess the box, trying to decipher the contents before opening it. This is the best part about receiving gifts. The guessing game, finding out if you were right—these are the things that make gift giving and receiving so exciting.

As I stare at my present, I think about the last time I received a gift, but I cannot think of a time. Every year, around my birthday, my mother would surprise me with breakfast and homemade *tres leches* cake, a traditional Spanish milk cake, but that was it. She always told me she never gave me presents because she did not want me to be reliant on material treasures.

If only she understood the only things I ever received that I cherished were my silver cross necklace and my stake, both given to me by my father. I never cared about fancy electronics or clothes. Still, it would have been nice to have received *something*.

I grab the sides of the box, using both my hands to hold it. The box is thick. It takes my full grasp to keep it on my lap without Jasik's assistance. I do not think about the fact that this might just be because I am literally this weak now. Maybe it has come to a point when I can barely hold on to a simple box.

Furrowing my brow, I shake the box around, listening as something inside moves. Jasik chuckles beside me, but I ignore him. I probably seem very childlike right now, but I do not care. I am having fun—for once.

"It sounds . . . soft," I say, even though I am not really speaking to anyone in particular. Still, I make my mental notes aloud for all to hear.

"It might be," Jasik responds, trying his best to be as vague as possible. It is only slightly annoying.

I shake it again, and something moves. I gnaw on my lower lip, trying to guess the contents without actually opening the box.

"You know, if you just open it—"

"Hush," I say, interrupting him as I continue my mental assessment.

What would Jasik get me? When did he even have time to buy something? I do not remember him ever leaving the manor except for his patrols, and I can't imagine him ignoring his duty to go *shopping*. I wonder if Hikari has confided in him my requests. My heart sinks a little. I do not know why I am ashamed, but I am. I hate that I have to cake makeup on my skin to feel . . . pretty, normal, just like my old self.

There is a bright crimson-colored ribbon wrapped around the box. It is twisted into a perky, full bow at the center. The color reminds me of Jasik's eyes—and of blood. I swallow hard, feeling my pulse race as I think about my formerly liquid diet. I do not crave blood the way I used to, but I desire the way it made me feel when I drank it. I have not felt that . . . power, that yearning since I hexed my coven.

Slowly, I unravel the bow. The ribbon is so silky smooth, it glides from the box the way blood drips down skin. I lick my lips as I remember the way it would coat my mouth as I drank deeply.

When one strand is free, I unravel the other one, twisting until the ribbon falls from my hands and lands in a heap on the floor. Jasik scoops it up, placing it on my bed beside him. He watches me intensely, his eyes a bright, fiery red. I feel my pulse race, my skin burning.

I wiggle the lid free, letting it fall to the floor as I stare at the contents. This time, Jasik does not clean up my mess. He stares fiercely as I take in his gift.

I suck in a sharp breath, my eyes burning at the sight. Placed inside the box are four things. One pair of black boots, already laced and ready for my feet to simply slide inside. The other is a black, military-style jacket, folded neatly, the cusp of the leather pristine and shiny. Atop that is a sparkly chain, and beside that is another box, sleek and black. I have seen all of these items before.

I run my hand over the boots, letting my fingertips graze each curve until I reach the jacket. I grab on to the fabric, squeezing it so tightly in my hand, my knuckles turn white. When I release it, I sit back and meet Jasik's gaze, swimming with emotions I can barely keep them in check.

"They are exactly the same," I whisper to him.

He smiles softly, nodding. "It took longer than I anticipated, but I found everything you lost that day."

"How? When? Why . . . " I trail off. So many questions are fluttering through my mind. I do not know where to begin.

"I know how important these were to you, and after you . . . " Jasik sighs. "These are not simply clothes, Ava. Like your necklace and your weapon, they are extensions of you. When you wear them, you become more confident in yourself. That confidence is what you are lacking now. It is what you are missing. You are still that same girl I met that night. You just do not see yourself the way I do. I think this might help."

I swallow the knot that forms and sniffle. I turn away from Jasik and stare at his gift to me. He is not simply gifting me clothes and shoes and jewelry. He is giving me back everything I lost that night.

After Liv died and I cursed my coven, I walked away from them, intent on never returning. I ignored their pleas as I put more and more distance between us. Eventually, they fell silent. I did not hear their cries or their screams for me to return, to reverse the spell. They were angry, but most importantly, they were pained.

I know that agony, because when they severed the vampire from the witch, I felt it too. That hollowness, that emptiness, that feeling of uselessness. I lived with those very emotions the day they used black magic against me. It was their time to suffer now. They needed to understand my desperation.

But the moment I returned to the manor, with the vampires in tow, I still felt...broken. I did not like who I became or what the witches made me do. Because when I spelled them, I cursed myself in that very same breath. Now, the vampire really is gone. I did not simply suppress the vampire or the witch, I stifled them. I silenced them. I became human in a world doused with magic.

That night, I stripped from my clothes, I tossed them in a waste bucket, and I set them on fire. The vampires surrounded me, watching in awe as I severed my very last links to my family. I ripped my cross from my neck and threw it in the fire too. I dropped my stake into that bucket, and I never looked back.

But now, these things stare back at me. My cross glistens in the low lighting, positioned directly beside a thin, black box.

"I was able to find a similar cross, chain unbroken, but that is your same stake," Jasik confides.

Confused, I look up at him, frowning. "How? How did you manage this? *When* did you do this?"

"After you went to bed that night, I cleaned up the mess, emptying the bucket. The stake was unharmed. Dirty from soot but otherwise okay. I cleaned it off and stored it, hoping, in time, you would ask me to get you another one. I always planned to return it to you when you asked for it."

"But I never asked for it back," I admit.

"I know, but I could tell you yearned for it. These things are part of you, and that scares you because you think you are different now. You think you are no longer a warrior, but you are. You are still *you*. You are still that strong, confident, smart, beautiful girl who looked at me and asked me to turn you into the very creature you feared most. All because you were willing to offer the only thing you had left to save your family. You have always been fearless and selfless, Ava, even now. Even when you are scared."

"You saved it for me?" I ask, awestruck. "And you still replaced these things for me? Even after all this time, you still believed I would come to my senses and want them back?"

"I knew you needed them, even if you did not, and I was willing to wait for you," he says. "After speaking with Will, I knew this was the time to return them. I wanted you to have everything you need while you make your decision."

My heart swells, tears threatening to fall. Jasik is right. I *did* need this. Like any good superhero with a cape and costume, I needed these clothes. They were my armor. Whenever I dressed in them and went out patrolling, I felt confident and safe, like these clothes alone provided some form of essential protection against my enemies. They did not, of course, but I was able to convince myself otherwise without even trying.

"I will not ask you to complete Will's spell," Jasik says. "I will not ask you to join me in this eternal life. And no matter what you choose, whether you get your powers back or not, I will support you, and I will protect you until my dying breath."

"Do you want me to complete the spell?" I ask, even though I know the answer.

Jasik is silent for a moment. He frowns, letting his gaze fall. When he finally looks at me again, his eyes are heavy.

"I want you to make this decision for yourself, not for me or for Will or for anyone else. It is important that you are happy with your decision, because whatever you choose will alter your life forever. I just hope you know that regardless of your decision, I will be happy, and I will always be here for you."

I drop the box, letting the contents fall onto the ground in a messy heap. I lean over, pulling Jasik to me, guiding his lips to mine. I run my hand through his hair, tangling my fingers in the locks, bunching the strands within my fists as I grip to hold him tighter, terrified he might pull away, even though I know he would never risk this connection. We might be a broken pair, but our bond is still there.

The moment our lips touch, something sparks within me. Jasik makes me feel safe when he is near, but I also feel *whole*. Never have I felt such intense love for another person before. I know Jasik will die for me; he would kill for me. Our bond is true and strong—something no curse or hex or black magic could ever break.

I moan as I move closer to him, enjoying his scent, his taste. He smells like cinnamon and summer air, and he tastes like mint and blood. I do not crave it the way I used to, but it tastes delectable on his breath. I could lose myself in Jasik's embrace, and that is the only darkness I welcome. Jasik is a beacon of light—one that will forever chase away the shadows.

Jasik pulls me close, and I open for him, resting my legs on either side of his as I straddle his lap. He mumbles my name breathlessly before he kisses me again. I love the way he speaks to me, the way he softly touches my skin, making sure he never hurts me, making me feel strong and beautiful, powerful with him beside me. I crave every part of his embrace.

He lifts me in his arms and stands, spinning around so he can place me gently on my bed. He is hovering over me, his eyes burning brightly against his pale, smooth skin. The crimson pools of his irises look almost neon now.

I kiss him again, nibbling playfully on his lip, and he laughs softly, exposing his fangs. My heart races when I see them, an ever-constant reminder of what I have lost.

As Jasik holds me, kissing me softly, whispering promises as bursts of air from the ceiling fan brush against my exposed skin, I lose myself in him, in his embrace, in his touch, in his taste. Always gently, Jasik never rushes me, allowing me to explore my emotions and desires only when I am ready.

When his cool skin brushes against my own burning desires, I know everything will be okay. As long as Jasik and I are together, love will always prevail. I tell myself my world is not crumbling, the witches are not prey to vengeance, and everyone I love is safe and happy. We are not at the brink of war. I have not lost my powers. In Jasik's arms, he reminds me that I am beautiful and strong and precious.

I lose myself in Jasik because I know that is the very place I will find myself again. His devotion, his love, his desires all match my own. With each touch, with each kiss, I feel the weakened parts of my soul grow stronger. Every moment of pain is consumed by him. He withstands the brunt of that fury so I do not have to, leaving me only with the euphoric experience of having him so near.

And when Jasik tells me he loves me, I say it back. Because I do love him. From the very depths of my soul to the fleshy curves of my heart, I am utterly in love with Jasik. I think I loved him the very first time I saw him. I loved him the moment he flashed his crimson eyes at me and promised he could save my life. Even back then, I think he loved me too.

I think that is why he risked everything to save me that

night. It scares me to know Jasik has wormed his way into my heart, because the harder I love him, the greater the pain will be when I lose him.

Hours later, when I wake, Jasik is still lying beside me, but he is not sleeping. He is resting behind me, body pressing against my own. Using his fingertips, he traces invisible designs along my bare skin. I shiver under his soft touch. He leans forward and kisses my skin gently where he was just touching.

I turn around to face him. I am lying on my back so I can see him more clearly. Jasik is perched up on an elbow, using one hand to hold his head upright while the other caresses my skin.

In this light, he is beautiful. I smile at him, but he does not see me. He is too busy focusing on his artwork. I giggle when he brushes a particularly sensitive spot, and I glance down, finally seeing my body through his eyes.

I suck in a sharp breath as I stare at the tiny black veins that coat my skin. Internally chastising myself for being so stupid, I tear my gaze away from the secrets I have been keeping to meet Jasik's eyes. He looks at me now, not bothering to hide the pain there.

"I am sorry," I whisper, knowing those words will fall flat. While I *am* sorry, I am not sorry for the right reasons. I am not sorry I kept the secret. I am only sorry he found out before I was ready to tell him.

The vampires know I am getting worse. I am thinning, my vision is blurry, I am not as hungry as I once was, I fall far too often, I get dizzy spells when I stand, I vomit a tarry substance that seems to *move* on its own... The list goes on and on. But for some reason, I have been hiding this small part of my transition. The worst part is I do not even know *why* I felt the urge to keep it a secret from Jasik. I just ... did.

"Why didn't you tell me?" Jasik asks, clearly hurt. His fingers trace the sprawling patterns, as if they are merely tattoos spanning my skin.

"I don't know," I whisper. My voice breaks as I speak.

I know this is not the answer he wants to hear, but he does not push it further. Instead, we sit in silence, both staring at my disfigured body, both wondering how much longer I have to consider my options before this evilness inside of me steals my choices from me. I only have so much time before the darkness will win.

We are still, both afraid to speak but equally afraid to break this moment, to walk away and pretend it never happened. This is important. We must talk about it. But we are both too scared to be the one to admit just how serious my situation has become.

A crashing noise jolts us awake. Before I can react, Jasik is out of bed, throwing on his clothes. He reaches the door in the blink of an eye, but before Jasik leaves, he turns back, like he is seeing me for the first time.

I blink again, and he is beside me. He thrusts his lips against mine. His kiss is rushed and hard; his lips smack against me almost painfully. I am still forming a kiss by the time he is pulling away.

"Get dressed," Jasik orders. "It is not safe here."

I nod, pulling the covers even tighter around me, as if they can protect me from what is happening downstairs. Someone screams, a heart-piercing bellow that ends abruptly.

The manor is silenced. I glance at the bedroom door and then back at Jasik, my heart beating so fiercely, it is painful. My chest burns, my throat dry. I have never been so terrified in my life.

I watch as Jasik is torn between leaving my side to aid the vampires and staying with me, to protect me from whatever might come crashing through my bedroom door.

"You must go," I say to him, even though the words physically pain me, as if they lash out, slicing through skin.

Again, Jasik looks from the door and back to me. I imagine he is playing through different scenarios of how he can make this work—as both the manor's protector and my lover—but each idea falls flat. There is no magic cure. He cannot be in two places at once. Jasik must choose, as much as it pains him to do so. And I do not want him to choose me.

"Go!" I shout.

Jasik flinches. Once again, my words lash out—this time at him. His eyes are wide, but I still see the pain behind them. He cannot hide his emotions, especially not from me. Not now. Not after last night.

"They need you," I say. My voice is screechy and raspy as panic envelops me in its sweet embrace.

"You are more important," Jasik admits.

"You cannot protect me if everyone else dies," I say. My reality is harsh, but it is true. What if Jasik is the deciding factor here? What if he alone can prevent the tables from turning?

"Promise me you will not leave this room," Jasik says. "You will not open that door for anyone but me. Promise me, Ava." His voice is hard and loud. He tries to hide his emotions, but I hear the panic in his words.

"I promise," I say, and I do mean it.

And with that, he is gone. The door slams behind him, and I envision him disappearing down the hall and leaping down the stairs, landing in the sitting room and engaging in a battle I should also be fighting. I do not know what is going on, but I am confident the witches are yet again waging war. I just hope the vampires can beat them without me.

The constant thumping of feet slamming against hardwood echoes all around me. Someone is running down the hall, and when the intruder reaches my bedroom, the noise stops. My door opens, and I shriek. Silenced only when I see Malik's face. His eyes are hard as his vision sweeps over me. I am still in bed, clutching the sheets as a cocooned shield of protection around my naked body.

Malik tears his gaze from mine and scans the room. Without a word, he exits, slamming the door behind him. Again, I hear footsteps until they fade away, the silence growing so loud, it hurts my head.

I am shaking, my teeth chattering painfully against each other. I do not know how much time has passed. Probably only minutes, but it feels like hours. I hear screaming coming from downstairs, their shrieks so vivid, it feels as though I am watching as their lives end right before my eyes.

I hate this. I hate that I am so weak, the vampires must offer their lives to protect me. Someone is waging war, and the vampires are fighting my battles while I sit in my room, cowering in the corner, praying no one finds me here. Because I can't protect myself. Not like this. Not when I can barely walk down the stairs without tripping. I am angry, and for once, I hate my life with a fiery passion.

With a renewed sense of purpose, I jump to my feet, yanking off the covers. A burst of cold air assaults my naked form, and I shudder as I make my way through my bedroom. I pull on clothes, whatever is within arm's reach. I run to my bedside, falling to my knees in a painful heap as I sift through the piles of sheets and blankets on the floor. Finally, I reach my present. I pull on my jacket and slip on my boots. I clasp my necklace around my neck and grab hold of my stake.

With a huff, I stand, chest heaving, heart burning, forehead slick with sweat from overexertion. My legs are shaky as I stand, and when I reach the door, I still. My hand hovers over the knob, and I gnaw on my lip. Suddenly, I am terrified of what I might find beyond this threshold—or what might find *me*.

"You can do this, Ava," I whisper, still shaken. "You have your armor now."

I glance down, taking in my attire. I might be skinnier, but I look like the same Ava, save for the veins covering my pale skin, which seem much more prominent when I am not hiding beneath oversize sweaters. My jeans are tight and tucked into my boots. My low-cut top is partially obscured by my jacket, but it does little to hide my body the way sweaters do. The moment I exit this bedroom, everyone will see. Everyone will know. But somehow, I do not care about that anymore, because I know they need me. *Jasik needs me.*

I exhale sharply, loudly, and I twist the handle, slowly exiting my room. My palm, which grips my stake, is drenched in sweat. I wipe it against my thigh. I am shaking so violently, I am certain our intruders will find me by that alone. The jingle in my bones, the thudding of my heart, will surely give away my location.

I glance back down the hall. I am several feet away from my bedroom now. Sliding against the wall, I take slow, deliberate steps toward the stairs.

I shriek when someone whips around the corner. The vampire ungracefully stumbles as she sees me, and she falls to the ground. She meets my gaze, her eyes wide with fear. Her face is splattered with blood, and she only looks at me for a second before she disappears in a blur.

I cast my attention back on the hallway before me. I wait only a second, but I hear nothing. No one seems to be chasing her, so I continue stalking forward. Still shaking, I try to squeeze my stake tighter, thinking that might calm my jitters. It does not.

When I reach the top landing of the stairs, I descend slowly. The noise from downstairs is much louder now, and while the sounds coming from the main level absolutely terrify me, it covers my own inner turmoil. So I welcome the screams, the thuds, the clear puff of a vampire combusting. Silently, I pray an enemy has fallen, not a comrade.

I reach the first landing and quickly spin on my heels, stepping backward until my back is flush against the wall. I hold my stake before me, fisting it with two hands. It shakes violently beneath my grasp, my arms growing more tired with each passing second. Slowly, I lower my weapon but keep both hands wrapped around the handle. Again, my palms are slick with sweat, and I know I should wipe them before my stake slips free. But I do not.

I take the first step, trudging slowly, only descending to the next when both feet are firmly planted on the first. It feels like an eternity passes by the time I am far enough down to peer into the sitting room.

As I take another step, I miss the planks, stepping awkwardly on the edge, and I teeter forward, losing my footing and stumbling down several stairs. I fall into a heap at the final landing. Only a few steps are before me now. I stare up from where I sit, catching the attention of everyone in the room.

I do not miss the surprise in my comrades' eyes. But their surprise is quickly suppressed by another, less friendly emotion: annoyance. Now, they must protect me *and* the other vampires *and* themselves.

I desperately want to help my friends. I want to protect the vampires and aid my allies. I watch, helplessly, as the others intercept every rogue vampire who spots me as easy prey.

As one charges, Jasik leaps forward, ignoring the vampire he was fighting in order to save me. With the rogue easily distracted by my mere presence, Jasik kills him swiftly.

My sire shoots me an angry glare, a silent order to go back upstairs, but I cannot move. Frozen in place, I watch as at least a dozen enemies terrorize everyone around them.

So many are dead, with dust coating the air and a sheer layer atop the furniture, and so many are wounded. Vampires who never faced the strength and fury of a rogue are forced to battle to the death, often losing to the superior predator.

Another is charging forward, but Jasik is nowhere to be seen. Lost in another room, likely cornered by even more attackers, he is gone, and I am alone. I look to the others for aid, but no one is close enough to save me. I must save myself.

The rogue vampire pounces, landing effortlessly atop me. He corners me in this place, where I am crouched helplessly on the floor, and as he looks at me, drool oozes down his chin, splattering on my cheek. I feel nauseated as his spit seeps down the sharp curve of my jaw and splashes onto my chest, but I do not wipe it away. I keep my gaze focused solely on him.

He looks at me the way a predator peers at prey. He knows I am not a threat to him. He does not see the witch or the vampire. He sees a *human*. He sees *food*.

He drops to his knees, and I take this moment to thrust my stake forward. Grunting loudly, even with both hands and using every bit of energy I have, the tip of my stake barely penetrates his sternum. One thing I never considered during my trek downstairs is how naturally strong rogue vampires are. Their bones are like solid steel. Even with my weapon, I never had a chance.

But as the vampire laughs and glances down at my feeble attempt to end his life, something happens. His eyes bulge from their sockets, and he releases a loud hiss before he combusts into ash. I cough, accidentally sucking in a sharp breath at the most inopportune time.

With the rogue gone, and as my vision begins to clear, I see Jasik. He must have used that brief moment to finish what I could not, using his own strength to pierce the rogue's heart with my stake. Jasik looks at me, still angry with my decision to disobey his order, before he turns and rejoins the fight.

Now, more than ever, I realize I will never again feel safe. Not from the witches, not from rogue vampires, not from this evil inside of me. I will never be safe as long as I remain powerless.

SIX

The rogue vampires are dead. I struggle to stand, hacking as I inhale ash. The air is hazy with particles that once formed our friends. We might have won this battle, but the cost leaves a heavy toll.

The vampires who survived are weak and wounded, bloody from waging a war they know nothing about. The hunters aid their nestmates, caring for the injured with bags of human blood.

I am still sitting on the final staircase landing. My bottom is planted firmly on the top step, and my feet dangle to the floor below. My elbows are resting against my thighs, and both my head and heart ache.

I replay the battle over and over again, and though I see it play out in my mind, all that remains is my fear. I am far too reckless for someone so weak. I realized this too late. The moment I nearly lost to the rogue vampire, I had a revelation.

I must complete the spell. I need my powers back. I am terrified of risking more magic, but I have no other choice. I am slowly losing my sanity, and as I slip further into the abyss, I will become more and more foolish with my actions. I may be only seventeen, but I must be wiser than *this*. The vampires deserve a champion, and lately, I am nothing more than a liability.

I scan the sitting room for Will, my only hope to become *normal* again, finding him in the solarium. He is aiding another vampire who is bleeding from a deep gash across his chest. His T-shirt is soaked through, the deep crimson stain penetrating the thin fabric and seeping down his torso. My stomach churns at the sight.

Will rips open a blood bag, spilling the precious healing elixir. He forces the opening into the vampire's mouth. Our wounded comrade drinks greedily, and with each slurp, he begins to heal—slowly but surely. Eventually, he will be okay.

The vampires are badly wounded, but those who made it this long will survive. Already, they are healing, and with the promise of fresh blood, they will be well again within a few hours. Tomorrow, it will be as if tonight's battle never happened. That is the beauty of being undead. Every new day practically erases the previous day's pitfalls. Their scars will mend, leaving nothing but sadness in their hearts as we mourn our losses.

"Ava," someone says, breaking my trance.

I tear my gaze from Will to see Malik standing beside me. His face is dusted in ash, and he is sweating. Dark streaks of cremains mixed with sweat drip down his forehead and cheeks. It looks like a bad makeup job, like Malik was taking lessons from me on how to conceal unwanted memories. I can even see where he wiped the film from his eyes.

My gaze trails his body. Malik is wearing sweatpants and a T-shirt. The rogue vampires caught us off guard. Most of the vampires were just waking, probably more slowly than usual thanks to last night's gathering with Will. The party meant they slept in later than usual, and our attackers used that to their advantage.

The rogue vampires' timing was perfect, and I can't help but wonder *how* they managed to pick the most opportune time to attack. How did they know we would be weak at that exact moment? How did they know that was the perfect time to risk an attack on a well-established nest? And *why*? Why now? Why us? We have not had any issues with rogue vampires since we cast them from Darkhaven months ago.

A tingle washes over my skin. It feels eerily like someone is watching me, but I brush off the sensation. Of course someone is watching me. Every vampire who survived the fight is staring at me as though this was my fault. Not being able to stand the accusations, I do not meet their gazes. I do not need them to make me feel even more responsible for this mess. If I was at my strongest, I might have been a real asset. Instead, I cowered in the corner, waiting to be saved like some pathetic damsel in distress.

"Are you okay?" Malik asks.

I blink several times, rooting myself back into this reality. I need to stop losing myself in my mind. Things here are more important. I might not have been an ally when the vampires attacked, but I will be one now.

I nod, swallowing hard. My chest hurts, my head is throbbing, and my heart feels like it exploded hours ago. But I am okay. I survived—no thanks to me. If it were not for Jasik, I would have died today. I have always been rash in my choices, but I do not think I have ever been this risky before.

What is wrong with me?

Why do I feel like I have something to prove?

I glance up, noticing how Malik's gaze is focused on my chest. I look down to see what has caught his attention, sucking in a sharp breath as I stare at the tiny black veins coating my skin. They seem to have spread farther, wrapping themselves around my entire body, successfully squeezing the life from me. When I stare at them for too long, they move, so I look away, adjusting my jacket so it better covers my skin.

"Ava," someone else says. I glance over and watch as Amicia glides toward me as if she is floating, not walking. She moves so effortlessly, so confidently. I envy her fearlessness.

"Amicia..." I whisper, feeling deep regret for having nearly ruined everything by thinking I was strong enough to join this fight. Some of her vampires likely died because Jasik was focused on protecting me. Their blood is on my hands, and my hands are already stained in red.

As always, Amicia looks pristine and perfect, as if she were not just in the midst of a war. Dressed in tight black pants and a matching top, nothing about her looks as though she just battled to the death. Her hair is loose and flows around her shoulders, her eyes are lined with black liner, and her lips are painted with a deep-red shade of lipstick.

In fact, the only thing that betrays her recent involvement in this battle is her hands. Her dark, smooth skin is coated in ash. Her black fingernails are caked with debris, likely the remnants of recently departed rogue vampires. The fact that Amicia can enter a battle and still look beautiful afterward shows just how powerful she truly is. I would kill for that strength, that confidence, that *power*.

"You need to leave," Amicia says bluntly.

My heart drops to the floor. I do not look down, fearing I will find it splattered against the stairs. My chest feels hollow without its steady beats. My eyes swell, and my mouth runs dry.

Leave? I can't *leave*. I belong nowhere else. I have *nowhere* else to go.

"Go to your room," Amicia clarifies. "You are too great a temptation right now."

I glance past her, looking into the eyes of a dozen hungry vampires. The accusations I saw just moments ago are gone. No longer do I see hatred and blame. I see *hunger*. They are wounded, and I am human.

Even the eyes of the hunters are distrusting. They too fear their primal, innate desires will overtake their common sense. I experienced those same fears when I transitioned. I know how much it hurts to control your urges when all you want to do is submit to them.

"I hate this," I whisper to myself. I am not speaking to anyone specifically, but I know everyone in the manor hears my admission.

"Ava?" Will says, walking over confidently as he interrupts my conversations with the others. He left the wounded vampire to care for himself, because he sees my distress and has come to my aid, like any good friend would. "What is going on?"

"I hate that I can't even be around you guys without being nothing more than a temptation. A *burden*."

I meet Will's gaze, and something settles between us. I do not have to ask him to follow me. I do not have to explain my interest in his knowledge of the reversal spell. The mere seconds of time that spans between us says everything I need to say. He nods sharply, and I stand. I walk away, retreating with Will following close behind.

We enter my bedroom, and I slam the door shut behind us. The seconds that pass as we remain silent feel more like hours. There are so many things I want to ask him about this spell, but I know we do not have a lot of time. And I am scared. I am fearful of what this spell might require. Severing a black arts curse cannot be easy magic.

"Are you sure this is what you want?" Will asks before I even have a chance to speak.

I nod feverishly. "I can't stand feeling this way. I am too weak to live in this world. Either I need to restore my powers, or I need to exit it completely." I do not clarify what the latter part would entail, but I know Will understands me.

"You are a lot of things, Ava, but weak is not one of them," Will says.

"You do not understand. You have your powers back. You do not know what it is like to sit here, fearing for your life as a rogue vampire drools all over your face and licks his lips. You do not know the mind-numbing fear that wraps around you when you know you are about to die. It was suffocating, Will. *Everything* about that battle was painful. I was forced to sit and watch as others risked their lives to protect me. *Me*. A former hybrid. One of the most powerful creatures on the planet! I should have been an asset, not a risk."

I am pacing my room, shouting even though I know the vampires downstairs can hear me. They are involuntarily eavesdropping due to my volume, listening as I confide in Will my deepest insecurities and worst regrets. But I do not care about them. I only care about the spell, about returning to my former self.

"I can't feel this way anymore," I confide. "I can't do nothing while my friends are butchered in front of me."

Will nods. "Okay. We can do the spell. Holland has already said he will help. We were just waiting for you to agree."

I swallow hard, my pulse suddenly racing. I still do not

know what it entails, and I am terrified to ask. I figure this is one of those moments when knowing too many details will work against me, so instead of asking about the ritual, I make a confession.

"I am scared."

"I know," Will says.

He walks over to me and takes my hands, bringing my palms to rest against his chest. I look up at him, staring in awe at how wonderful he has been these past several weeks. Will has given up his life to help me restore my powers. He has known me only a fraction of the time, yet he has shown me more devotion than my own mother.

"I promise everything will be okay," Will says softly.

His crimson irises are bright and big, and they do not hide his fear, even as it mirrors my own. I know he is happy that I have decided to partake in this ritual, but it comes at a cost. Everything in Darkhaven comes at a cost.

"Is it dangerous?" I ask, silently begging him to lie to me.

"Isn't all magic dangerous in some way?" Will says, avoiding my question.

"And you are sure you can complete the ritual?" I ask. My mouth runs dry as I wait for his response.

"With Holland's help, yes."

I sigh heavily, sharply, and then I inhale long and slow. I take deep breaths, steadying my nerves, readying myself for this next moment. Because after this, nothing will ever be the same.

I meet Will's gaze again, and this time, I am determined. I do not speak, and nothing about my actions betrays just how frightened I truly am. Once again, I agree to submit myself in every way to magic.

"Tomorrow. We complete the spell tomorrow."

The night air is cool against my skin. It is nearly spring, but winter has yet to make way for warmth. The snow is melting, but at night, when the temperature drops, what has melted freezes over. Now, Darkhaven is coated in a frozen layer of murky sludge. This is not exactly prime ritual weather, especially considering my inability to withstand the frigid temperatures.

I shiver as a cold breeze assaults my nearly nude body. I am dressed in a traditional Wiccan cloak. It is ruby red and stands out beside the dark night sky. Beneath my robe, I am wearing only a sports bra and spandex shorts. The ritual calls for me to be sky-clad, but I refused. It is far too cold for me to be completely naked.

Holland and Will are dressed similarly. They both wear matching ruby-colored robes, and they are topless beneath them. When they move, I see their toned chests. Will seems unaffected by the bitter temperature, but Holland is clearly as affected as I am. His cheeks look raw, his nose pink, and his eyes are watery.

To complete this ritual, we are outside the manor, standing in the front yard. I teeter on the stone walkway that leads from the wraparound porch to the forest beyond the manor. The hunters gather on the porch, watching with Amicia as Holland and Will prepare.

Ready and eager to begin, I am at the center of a pentagram drawn in the snow with blood. At each point of the star, there is an altar with items and cherished relics to represent each of the five elements.

Much like the vampires, I too am completely unsure of this process. I did not ask Will for details, because I knew this ritual would come at a cost. For me to break the spell and regain my place within this vampire nest, I will likely need to do things I would not do otherwise. He and I agreed it would be better if I go into the spell unaware of what is required of me. All I can do now is hope for the best.

The wind picks up, blowing my tresses into a ragged heap at my shoulders. Something catches my eye, and I glance over. It is silky and smooth, shiny and bright red. On one of the altars, I see the crimson ribbon Jasik used to wrap my gift. I smile as I stare at it before I search the onlookers for my sire.

Jasik is standing beside Malik and the others. His broad shoulders are cast back as he stands tall and stares into the distance. I follow his gaze, spotting nothing but dead, snow-covered trees. I am certain we are alone tonight, but the hunters are strapped with weapons and prepared to defend this ritual space during our most vulnerable moments.

"Ava, are you ready to begin?" Holland asks.

I tear my vision away from the forest to find his gaze. I smile at him, feigning confidence, but inside, my heart is pounding in my chest. Holland is the only one I can fool tonight. The others cannot only sense, but also hear, how nervous I feel.

"I am," I say loudly.

Holland and Will are standing just inside the circle that surrounds the pentagram star. Both stand on either side of the northernmost point—the one that represents spirit. The pentagram and the circle that connects the elements, forming one constant energy source, are all lined in the snow with blood. Amicia was kind enough to allow us to use bags from her personal supply to form our circle tonight. I try not to stare at it too long. The stark contrast between the plush white snow and the deep-red blood makes me queasy—yet another feeling I cannot wait to lose when I return to my former self.

"This ritual will not be easy," Holland says. He looks away from me and toward the vampires. "At no time are we to be disturbed. No one is to break our circle. Understand?"

Holland looks from vampire to vampire—from Jasik to Malik to Hikari to Amicia, finally landing his gaze on Jeremiah, who remains emotionless. I watch as Amicia nods sharply, but Holland is distracted, not looking at her. He does not see when she agrees to his terms. Instead, he watches his boyfriend closely before finally clearing his throat and looking back to me.

"We will begin by invoking the elements," Holland says. "Ava, you are standing at the center of the most powerful witch symbol: the pentagram. Each point of the star represents one of the five elements: earth, water, air, fire, and spirit. The circle connects each element because you must harness each to work as one if you wish to restore your powers and sever the link to your former coven."

My nerves are rapid firing as I listen to him. I feel giddy, excited to know I am only moments away from harnessing the elements, something I feared I would never again do. My enthusiasm for the spell calms my nerves, and I am no longer worried about the sacrifice this ritual will inevitably entail. There is only me, this spell, and the moment I am made whole again.

"Turn away from us and face the point at the southwest corner," Holland orders.

I obey, my gaze landing on the altar positioned at the very edge of the bloodstained point. I know this corner is meant to represent the earth element. I peer at the tree stump that serves as both this corner's altar and a representation of the element. Atop the cleanly sliced wood is a pentacle necklace, gold and silver coins, stones, a dish of salt, a cauldron with dried herbs, and several green candles.

"Earth is everywhere," Holland begins. "A passive element, she is often overlooked, but she is by far the superior element. Though she does not harness the active power that comprises the other elements, earth grants us the one thing the others cannot: life. Earth births us and sustains us on this physical plane. Earth encompasses and carries all magic in her womb. She provides nourishment and protection, prosperity and rest. She offers both plant and animal life, without which we would perish."

I close my eyes, letting Holland's words wash over me. My legs are buzzing as I imagine the power and strength of the earth seeping through the soles of my shoes and into my feet. I am rooted in place as Mother Earth revitalizes all the broken parts of me. When I am scared, when the darkness swirling within me begins to awaken, earth stabilizes me, allowing me a much more powerful force to lean on in this time of need. With earth by my side, I already feel stronger, more confident in my ability to vanquish this evil.

"Turn to the east, where the water element awaits your connection," Holland says softly.

When he speaks, I do not hear him through my ears. He speaks *through* me, as if his voice echoes within the depths of my soul. I obey his command, turning mindlessly to the east.

I open my eyes, allowing my gaze to linger on the offerings bestowed before me. The altar here is formed by compact, frozen snow. The shards of icicles are compressed together, forming a mound with a smooth surface for the ritual offerings. A silver chalice filled to the brim with slowly melting snow sits atop the heap, as well as a scrying bowl, a crystal sphere, seashells, driftwood, a mirror, and a blue candle.

"Water is a partner to the earth, as she aids her sister element in promoting life. Like earth, water appears gentle in nature, but she contains immense power. She cleanses and calms while healing our bodies and nourishing our minds. Water governs magic over love and emotion, intuition and pleasure."

I close my eyes as the air becomes heavy with mist. I shiver as the temperature drops, the cool night breeze turning almost icy. Even though I am cold, I feel rejuvenated. I feel stronger than I have in weeks. Connecting to two of the five elements has left me with a renewed purpose, and my excitement to continue this ritual is steadily building. I fear I might actually burst from the frenzy.

"Turn to the west, and connect with air," Holland continues.

I open my eyes, swiftly turning on my heels to face the proper direction. I am facing the forest now, but I keep my sights set on the altar before me. Formed by stacking books, the altar is adorned with an athame dagger, a feather, a bell, incense that burns steadily into the night, a bright crimson ribbon, and a yellow candle.

"As air passes over the still earth, the world begins to move. Air offers consciousness to all things that call the earth home. Air is the element of communication and ideas, exchanges that are necessary for life to thrive. Unlike the other elements, air is invisible. We are only aware of air through his effects. Close your eyes to completely connect with the element."

I obey, closing my eyes. Suddenly, a burst of air swirls all around me, rustling my hair, nearly pushing me over with its ferocity.

"Air moves swiftly," Holland whispers. "It is the only element that changes as it is influenced by the other elements. Fire makes it warm, almost too hot to bear. Water makes it hazy, frosty, dangerously cold. Air is ever-changing and always self-aware—two qualities you must encompass if you wish to restore your powers."

I nod, keeping my eyes closed as I hold my arms out to my sides. I smile as the air brushes against my skin, working its way through the fabric of my cloak until it caresses my bare skin.

"Turn to the southeast corner," Holland orders.

I open my eyes as I turn, and I face the fire altar. Stacks of firewood bundled together for the altar, with a smooth surface made from a large tile. Flames decorate every inch of it, the bright streaks of paint almost glowing in the moonlight. Atop the altar there is a wand, matches, thorns from a cactus, a pile of ash, dragon's blood oil, and a red candle.

"Fire's power is pure and strong. This element is often considered the most powerful and the most useful of the five. Fire is primal and dangerous. He invokes both life and death. In fire, we find passion and safety, much like the warrior's spirit. Fire is courageous and destructive. It both destroys and renews everything it touches."

The air sizzles around me, ignited by fire's warmth. I welcome it even when it becomes hard to breathe. I feel the heat deep within my bones, but it stifles the chill. In a moment, when I must release the element, the burst of cold air will settle over me again, and I will miss the heat. Sweat beads at my temple, and my chest heaves as I struggle to breathe.

"Return north and face us once again, where you will connect with the spirit element," Holland says.

Reluctantly, I spin to face him, but I do not watch him. Once again, my sight lands on the offerings he has put out for me. This time, there is no altar. Each item that represents the spirit element is placed on the ground and forms a complete circle at the very tip of the pentagram. There is a golden crown adorned with crystals, a third-eye jewel, a small glass doe, several quartz crystals, a spiral wheel relic, and a white candle.

"Spirit is the bridge between the physical and the spiritual, between the material and the celestial realms. Spirit connects the body and soul, forming one unique being. All the elements work together, commanded by spirit, to become one within you."

Slowly, the elements I released spark to life once again, forming a complete circle within my core, fueling my desire, rejuvenating my strength. I am no longer cold or hot. I am perfectly sated, utterly at peace in this brief moment in time.

"Do you feel the connection, Ava?" Holland asks. "Listen as each element speaks to you. Obey their command. Submit to their strength."

"Yes," I say, breathing heavily. "I am connected."

The bliss swelling within my heart is almost too much to bear. I spent weeks on my deathbed, simply waiting for time to stop, for the darkness to take over. I lost myself the day I hexed my coven, and it has taken far too long to find my joy again. This moment, when I am reunited with the elements I so desperately crave, I am elated. I am at peace. The emptiness is gone, and though the darkness remains, I feel stronger. I feel as though the evil is no match for my fury.

I open my eyes, and Holland and Will are no longer standing at the tip of the pentagram. They are mere feet before me. Both dressed to match me, they shimmy free, removing their garments to reveal their bare chests.

"It is time now, Ava," Holland explains.

Will snaps his fingers, and all five candles—one for each element—is lit aflame. The ritual has officially begun.

"Relinquish your hold over the moon," Holland orders. "Reverse your spell."

Shaking and heavy with fear, I look at the moon. I stretch out my arms beside me, angling my head upward so I can stare at her glory. She is bright white with splashes of gray, almost iridescent against the black, starry sky. Her rays shine down upon us, illuminating our ritual space. She looks happy to abide by my wishes, like she has missed me as much as I have missed her.

I call to the moon, summoning her power, using the circle's magic and the elemental gain to reverse my spell. I chant loudly, clearly, carefully casting my spell so I may return to my former self once again. My Latin incantation swirls round and round in my mind and echoes all across the silent, sleepy land.

The trees come to life, swaying as the elements surge through the forest, rejuvenating even what has slumbered since the start of winter. The air is hot and misty, and the snow at my feet quickly melts away. I sink into the earth, the mud coating my shoes as I plunge into its depths.

The moment I complete the spell, I feel the moon release me. Her hold over my soul dissipates, and raw, pure magic courses through me once again. The evil residing inside of me springs to life, latching on to my magic, sucking the life from it like a leech. I keel over, caught by Will, who struggles to keep me upright as I scream in utter agony.

With my magic restored, the darkness has found a new purpose. It feeds on my strength, using it to become more powerful. Slowly, it outshines even me, even as I desperately grab on to the elements, refusing to relinquish them until the darkness evaporates.

"We need to complete the severing spell!" Will shouts.

I am holding too tightly on to the elements, and the wind is howling now. It experiences my pain, and it screams. Will bellows over it, trying to get the attention of Holland, who is busy chanting his own spell. I do not understand the archaic language he is speaking, and I am too distracted by the gut-churning, stabbing pain in my core to concentrate on his words.

I fall to my knees as Will leaves my side. When I scream again, the earth shudders. In the distance, I hear something rumble, and I look up in time to see the frozen tundra split in two, an echoing vibration that worms its way up my spine. I know I have done this, but I cannot release the elements. Not yet. Not until the severing spell is complete. Without their aid, I will fall victim to the evil inside.

Someone grabs on to my arm and yanks it forward. I glance up in time to see Will. I smile at him, but he is not looking at me. The flash of something silver distracts me momentarily, and then I watch as the blade slices into my arm.

I shriek, screaming so loudly I am certain I have woken all of Darkhaven. Will releases my arm, but only when he has dug so deeply, I will certainly bleed out in only minutes.

He twists the blade in his hand and uses it to slice into his own flesh. He slaps our wounds together and sinks into the earth as I do. Together, we hold on to each other. Both unmoving, unspeaking, focusing solely on Holland, who still stands over us. His arms are stretched out before us as he recites his spell, chanting the same sentences over and over again.

Will whispers softly, so quietly I almost do not hear him. I watch his lips, my eyelids growing heavy, but the roaring wind silences him. His eyes are closed, his hand grasping my arm, his fingers digging painfully deep into my flesh.

His blood is pouring from his wound, dripping steadily into my gaping arm. I have performed a bloodletting spell before, but it never felt like this. Silently, I pray these two know what they are doing, and that by combining my blood with Will's, we are not invoking a worse evil.

"Ava! Look at me!"

Holland sounds so far away. When I turn to face him, everything feels heavy. It takes every ounce of energy I have to open my eyes and stare into his. His irises are murky and brown. They are puddled messes swarming with tears.

"Drink," Holland orders.

Only then do I notice his arm before me. His wrist has been slashed, and blood seeps from the thin sliver of a wound. I lick my lips and never question his order, even as I press my mouth to his arm and suck.

Holland is still chanting. With every passing second, I hear him better, yet his voice grows quieter. It is an odd sensation—one that alerts me to other things.

The smell of blood is heavy in the air. It coats it in a thickness, making it hard to breathe. I continue slurping down Holland's offering, ignoring the steady thumps of his heart, even as they grow weaker by the second.

The more I drink, the hungrier I feel. When Will falls away, slumping to the ground, his eyes fluttering into unconsciousness, I ignore him, pushing him away in favor of the witch.

Holland's blood coats my tongue. He tastes like the elements, if the elements actually had a flavor. He tastes like the earth and fire and water and air. If all four mixed together, they would taste just like Holland.

Only when he shudders his last breath and the echoing pulse of his heart ceases do I finally stop. I pull away, releasing Holland, who long ago fell limp in my arms. When I drop him, he falls to the ground in a heap beside Will.

Both men stare back at me, eyes lifeless, yet somehow full of accusations.

I did this. I killed my friends.

SEVEN

I am lying on my back, staring up at the stars. The moon shines brightly above me, her rays cascading down, brushing against my skin. I was right; she missed me too. I can feel it as she looks down at me now. Once again, I am a child of the night, and I have returned home to her.

I do not move. Instead, I assess what just happened. The spells cast and ritual performed were powerful but weakening. Yet, I feel more alive than ever before.

Everything tingles, from the soles of my feet to the top of my head. From root chakra to crown, I am reborn. Again.

I have waited so long to be reunited with my former self, to once again feel the power of the vampire and magic of the witch.

The salty air fills my lungs with its tantalizing fragrance, and I scrunch my nose at it. It has been far too long since I experienced the nearby sea. I listen as waves crash against the rock wall separating the woods from the water. When I close my eyes, I swear I can even hear fish swimming within its depths.

The frozen tundra, which holds me now, is hard and unyielding. After months of hibernation, it feels as stiff and uncomfortable as my muscles. It roots me in place, the cold seeping into my bones, but I do not fear it. Not anymore.

Something in the distance catches my attention. The tiny hairs covering my exposed skin alert me to a presence, and the sound of creatures scurrying in the woods, fluttering out of sight, fills my mind. I know they surround us. Animals find protection in these woods just like the vampires. We share this space, never venturing too close. We remain at a distance from all life—humans *and* animals alike. I suppose we have temptation to thank.

I do not move. I simply lie still, allowing each sensation to take hold of my body, but the moment I allow myself reflection, the reality of my situation swarms at once, filling me with anxiety. My mind is ablaze with my deepest fear and my everlasting regret.

I roll over, grunting as I move to peer at those around me. While I was lying mindlessly in the shadows, enjoying my newfound strength, my world came crashing down around me. And I didn't bother to care. I was too consumed by my own revelations and my strengthening hold over the pure, raw energy flowing through me.

My body is stiff, and my muscles ache as I attempt to stand. My legs feel like jelly, but I find my way to my feet. I teeter, trying to remain upright as I gasp at the sight before me.

The hunters are no longer standing on the front porch. But Amicia is there. Our fearless leader stands alone, casting her gaze upon me with a strange look on her face. She smiles, her eyes glowing with a hint of deviousness. I shudder and break eye contact as I search for my friends.

Both Will and Holland are cradled in the arms of others. Hikari holds her dripping wrist to Will's mouth, and he drinks greedily. Slowly, he is gaining strength. His wounds are healing.

Jeremiah holds on to Holland with such ferocity, I fear he

might break his boyfriend into pieces. I know he is careful, but he is also panicked.

Because Holland is unconscious.

I shriek at the sight of his lifeless body, limp in the hands of his lover. I stumble forward, falling quickly, but I am caught by Jasik, who wraps me in his arms. He holds me closely, his gaze assessing every inch of my body for imperfections, for signs the spell did not heal me.

"It worked," I whisper, and he pulls me into his arms.

All at once, his tension releases, and he nearly falls weak under my grasp. I never realized how much my situation affected him. Like the other hunters, Jasik is good at hiding his emotions if he chooses to. I guess he didn't want me to know how much it pained him to see me slowly lose my mind at the hands of black magic.

"Holland," I whisper into the crevice of Jasik's neck. I do not hide the pain in my voice. I am terrified to look away, but I cannot simply ignore my dying friend. I cannot just pretend Holland isn't battling for his life only a few feet away from where I sit now.

"He wanted this," Jasik says as he pulls away from me. Again, he carefully assesses my reaction. What is he searching for?

I frown. "What do you mean? He wanted what?"

Not bothering to wait for a response, I tear my vision from Jasik to look at Holland, who still has not moved.

Jeremiah is shaking, teetering back and forth as a frail, dying Holland lies still in his lap. Jeremiah says Holland's name over and over again, begging him to wake up so he can heal him.

I understand his predicament. If Holland is not conscious

when Jeremiah heals him, he will become a vampire. If Holland is both conscious and well enough to simply use the benefits of vampire blood, he will be healed and wake again as a witch. The timing must be perfect, and from the look of things, Holland might already be too far gone.

Jeremiah lays Holland's motionless body on the ground, straightening him quickly, and he begins chest compressions. He is muttering to himself about how Holland needs to be awake, his heart must be beating before he can drink vampire blood. I close my eyes, tears streaming down my face as I replay my own transition.

No one really knows how it works—how one becomes a vampire. No one really knows how some mortals are born witches and some are born humans. It just happens. For witches, there are bloodlines. Something makes us... different. You can't simply *become* a witch. You are either born one or you are not. You either can access magic or you cannot. It is that simple.

Vampirism is never simple. These moments are crucial. One minuscule mistake means the difference between mortality and immortality. Giving Holland blood at the very second his heart stops beating means he will awaken as a vampire. He will have died with vampire blood in his system. That is enough to change him.

At the same time, he doesn't have to die. At least, not like this. I remember my transition so vividly, it feels like only days have passed, not months. I was bled out by a rogue vampire and on the brink of death when Jasik saved me. By drinking from him, a vampire's blood consumed my system, overpowering my mortal blood and replacing it with... something else. With some strange mixture of *both* species. At some point, my heart must have stopped. I died as a witch, and I was reborn a hybrid.

I watch as the world falls silent. Jeremiah ceases chest compressions, and everyone freezes in place. Time slows, and we all listen. The weak, sputtering beats of a dying heart ring through the air, swirling in my mind.

Holland is alive.

Jeremiah moves quickly, understanding this is his only chance to heal him—hopefully without risking the change. He holds his bleeding wrist to Holland's mouth, but the blood simply fills the gape and splashes down his chin. Holland is not swallowing, because the dead cannot drink.

I scream an ear-piercing, heart-stopping bellow, and I fall to my knees. Jasik holds on to me, keeping me away so Jeremiah can finish his part of the ritual. I understand why the others did not clue me into these parts. If I would have known the cost would be Will or Holland, I never would have allowed us to go through with it. I would have accepted my fate and lived out the rest of my days in ignorant bliss.

Jasik soothes me as I crumble against him, watching as Jeremiah desperately tries to revive Holland. Every passing second, the dying witch becomes paler, and my heart lurches at the sight of him.

"You must drink, Holland," Jeremiah says, as if he can actually hear him. Holland's heartbeat is weak—so weak, I wonder if it is enough to keep him conscious. I worry we will not be able to save him, and if that's the case, I will never forgive myself if the cost for eternal life is his innocent soul.

I glance at Will, who is still feeding from Hikari. The spell must have taken too much of his strength, because he does not seem to be relying on his own innate healing abilities. He leans against Hikari, who holds him close as Will drains her power.

Finally, after far too many seconds have passed, Will moves to sit upright, pushing away Hikari's offering. She sits back, watching him carefully before finally stepping away to stand beside the other hunters. She wipes off her wrist, and the wound already begins to heal. Soon, there will be no trace of her offering to Will.

With a strange look on his face, Malik watches Jeremiah carefully. He does not look to me, and he does not offer his assistance to Jeremiah. Either the vampire will heal the witch—or he will not. There is nothing any of us can do but wait and hope that timing works to our benefit.

Will shimmies over to me and says something, but I do not understand his words. I am too focused on watching Jeremiah. He weeps now, because he understands it has been several minutes and Holland has not woken.

"Please, baby. Drink," Jeremiah whispers.

"Ava!" someone shouts, and I tear my gaze from Holland to look at Will. I blink several times to clear my vision. "Are you okay? How do you feel?"

I am silent for a moment as I consider his words. How *do* I feel? I feel fine. I feel *strong.* Magic and power are coursing through my veins, and for once, I can *feel* its presence. The darkness, the evil within my soul, is gone. When I close my eyes and search the depths of core, I do not feel it anymore. I reversed my spell and severed my link to the witches and their misdeeds, but at what cost?

I look at Holland again, and I notice the exact moment his eyes flutter. I gasp, shrieking for the others to look at him.

"He's awake!" I shout. "Feed him now!"

Jeremiah never moved his wrist, and for the past several minutes, he has continuously bled into Holland's mouth, so my order is moot. But I cannot help myself. I refuse to let Holland die. Not for me. Not for my cause.

When Holland opens his eyes, he blinks several times, likely clearing his vision. His eyes go wide when he finally settles on Jeremiah, who still hovers above him. Finally, Holland latches on to the blood offering, and I listen as he takes several deep swallows.

I sigh, sinking back against Jasik, who still cradles me in his arms. That was close—*too* close. Knowing Holland will be okay, I am able to focus on another emotion besides fear.

Anger.

I am absolutely, utterly, overwhelmingly *furious* with the vampires. How could they not tell me about this part?

"How did this happen?" I ask, breaking my gaze to stare at Will, who simply slumps backward. He no longer looks at me, because he is ashamed of what he did. I do not need to ask him to know this. I can see it written across his face—his pale, sickly face.

I let my gaze linger. Will's body is sluggish and weak. His frame is no longer toned and strong. He looks…frail and powerless.

What happened to him during this spell?

"Are you okay?" I whisper. I don't know why I am speaking so softly. Everyone around me, except for Holland, can hear our conversation. But still, I feel like Will is about to divulge something deeply personal, so I speak softly.

He looks at me, meeting my gaze, and that's when I see it. *Finally,* I see it. I was so distracted by Holland and being reborn, I didn't notice the most obvious change in Will's demeanor or presence.

His eyes are brown.

"Will . . ." I whisper, trailing off. I shake my head, and my eyes begin to swell. "Please tell me you didn't . . ."

"Didn't what?" Will asks, frowning, his forehead creasing into two deep lines. I don't remember that ever happening before.

"Tell me you did not take the darkness into you," I whisper. I am shaking, absolutely terrified of his answer. I know I need to hear it, but I worry his response will break me.

Will shakes his head. "I didn't. I promise I didn't."

"Then . . . how?" I ask.

Will smiles at me, and although he looks weaker than he ever has before, he also looks *happy*. In fact, I have never seen him look so peaceful, so . . . elated. I don't have to ask him to know he is comfortable with his decision, with his sacrifice. I just need to know what that is exactly. What did he give up in order for me to live again?

"What did you do?" I hiss.

"There needed to be a sacrifice, Ava," Will explains. "Black magic is meant to be irreversible, so reversing its effects comes at a cost."

"I don't understand," I say. While I am processing his words, I don't fully understand their meaning.

"The only way to complete the spell was for you to harness *more* magic. You needed to overpower the coven that cursed you, and there was only one way to do that," Will says.

"How?" I whisper.

"I spent a lot of time searching for answers to your problem," Will says. "When I finally found a spell that would work, I didn't stop there. I searched for something else—something that was meant for me but would also help you. And I found it, Ava. I finally found it."

"What did you find?" I ask. My pulse is racing as I wait for him to answer.

"Peace," he says simply.

"What does this mean, Will? What are you saying?"

"One part of the spell required a sacrifice," Will admits. "The *still-beating heart of a mortal victim* was your only path to immortality. But not just *any* mortal. You needed a witch, and we only knew of one."

I suck in a sharp breath, glancing over at Holland, who still drinks from Jeremiah. So far, he seems okay. His heart did stop, but he was brought back by chest compressions. That was a natural, *human* save, so he should be okay to drink. And now he is being healed.

Again, I remind myself that he should be okay. Because he *has* to be okay.

"Holland agreed to this spell," Will explains. "He *wanted* to do it."

Finally, Jeremiah looks up at me, and I do not mistake the anger there. He is seething, furious that his boyfriend would risk so much for me. I tear my gaze away, not wanting to see the hatred there. Jeremiah might care for me as he does any other familial bond, but he *loves* Holland. And if he dies, Jeremiah will never forgive me.

"And what about you?" I ask, glancing back at Will. "What was your part in this?"

"You needed a power source, and not just the strength of a single vampire. You needed something *more*."

"A hybrid," I whisper.

Will nods. "The spell was surprisingly specific. *The blood of neither mortal nor immortal.* My guess is a black magic curse was never meant to be broken. The reversal was supposed to be impossible. But eventually, such a creature came into existence."

"What does this mean for you?" I ask, swallowing the knot in my throat.

"It means I am finally free," Will says, smiling.

I notice Will is shivering. He wraps his arms around his chest, trying to keep the cold from claiming his life—his *mortal* life. I frown and shimmy out of my cloak. I hand it to him, and gratefully, he accepts it. I am wearing nothing but a sports bra and shorts, yet I feel fine. The cold does not bother me.

"You needed the blood of a hybrid, because that's where our magic comes from," Will says. "Our *blood* is that of both a vampire and a witch, and it makes us what we are. You were created by combining the two and being strong enough to fight both. You needed that strength to become stronger than those who cursed you."

"But what does that make you?" I ask.

"Human," Will says softly.

"And that's what you always wanted."

"It is. I'm not like you, Ava. I have no family, no friends. My sire killed everyone I ever cared about. After I escaped him, I spent far too many years searching for someone like me, someone who would *understand*. Do you know what it is like to be alone for that long? It's crippling, and I am tired." Will sighs loudly, sinking even further into himself.

He looks weaker than ever before, yet he looks content with his decision. He does not regret his actions or his sacrifice.

"But you have a home now," I say. "You belong here. With us."

"I appreciate you all, but it's not the same for me. I see the way they are with you. You truly have become one of them."

Will glances at Amicia, and she nods. "But I am a stranger—a welcomed stranger, but still a stranger."

I shake my head. "That's not true."

"It's okay, Ava. This is what I always wanted. I searched the earth three times over to find a coven smart enough to reverse your curse. When I finally found them, they had more answers than I could have ever hoped for. I owe them my life, because they helped me release my final burden: immortality."

"You are mortal," I say. This is obvious, but the words slip from me. It is almost as though I needed to speak them aloud to understand what has happened.

"I am," Will says, even though I wasn't really asking for confirmation.

"You will live and die a mortal life," I say. I don't want to think about that, so I cast out the visions in my mind.

"I will. Maybe I will finally find someone to spend my time with, now that I am more relatable," Will says with a chuckle.

"I'm sorry," I whisper. I hate the pain I have brought to these vampires. They have only tried to help me succeed in this life, and I have brought them nothing but sacrifice and misery.

Will shakes his head and says, "I'm not."

I stare at my reflection in the mirror and smile.

I am standing in the training quarters, a section of the manor I have not been in for quite some time. After I was cursed, I hated coming down here. This place was a constant reminder of the girl I once was—strong, confident, powerful. I was sure I would never again be that girl.

The room is long and rectangular, taking up at least half

the manor's basement. The mat flooring is squishy, and I sink into it as I try to maintain my balance. One of the long side walls is comprised of floor-to-ceiling mirrors, allowing sparring vampires to witness how their bodies move during certain attacks. Malik, my former trainer who was recently rehired, swears by this method.

I did not change after the ritual. My sports bra and spandex shorts are tight, and they barely cover my skin. While I wouldn't normally wear these clothes on patrol, I am excited to train in them.

It feels like years have passed since I last hunted rogue vampires, since I used my skill set to protect the humans of Darkhaven. I haven't patrolled the woods in weeks. Now that I am starting to feel like myself again, I am eager to return to my nightly ritual.

Still staring at my reflection, I smile as I spin in circles, hoping to catch glimpses of my body as I swirl around. I like the way I look when the light hits me just right, at the perfect angle when it illuminates my strength. I see muscle where there was only bone yesterday. I know I was withering away, succumbing to the darkness inside me, but now I am free. I wonder if this is how Will feels now that he is free from his curse too.

My skin has color again. I am no longer sickly pale. My eyes are crimson red, and my hair is shiny and lush. Over the weeks, my strands were lackluster, and I was losing handfuls at a time when I showered.

As I peer at my skin, now smooth and clear, the black veins are gone, and when I close my eyes, listening closely, I hear nothing. No darkness. No evil. Because I am no longer cursed.

I am free.

The best part about my transition back into a hybrid cannot be denied: I feel *strong*. I do not need to see my muscles flex to know I am as powerful now as I was the day I transitioned many months ago. I hated what I was back then. I desperately wanted to learn how to control my blood lust so I could return to the witches as a valued member of my coven. It is crazy to think how much has changed since then.

"Are you sure you're ready for this?" Malik asks, breaking my concentration. He is standing behind me, watching as I steal another glance at my healthy frame.

I do not face him. Instead, using the mirror, I nod excitedly, eager to begin. "I am."

After the spell was complete, Jeremiah was able to restart Holland's heart. His blood healed him, but he is still weak from harnessing enough magic to sever my link to the witches. Both he and Will are resting. They must recover, but I have never felt more alive.

Guilt rises in my chest, but I push it down. I must remind myself that I am immortal; they are not.

"I worry I'm rusty," I admit.

"Maybe we should wait," Malik says. "There is always tomorrow."

I smile at that because he's right. There *is* tomorrow. There will always be tomorrow now that I am once again a vampire. I curl my lips, exposing my teeth, as I lean against the mirror. I use my palms to hold myself upright so I can get close. I stare at my canines, which hang only slightly lower than they used to. They are low enough and strong enough to tear through flesh, and suddenly, I am overwhelmed by my desire to feed. My stomach rumbles, and I make a mental note to feed after training.

"The others needed to rest," Malik says. "Maybe you should take a day too. Just to be safe."

I shake my head, standing. I push myself off the mirror and turn to face him. I am annoyed by his insistence that I need to rest, but I do not show it. Malik might want to get rid of me tonight, but I am not going anywhere.

"We have bigger problems than my need for R and R," I say.

"Like what?" Malik asks.

"Rogue vampires attacked our nest for a reason. They might have died, but there are always more where they came from. Who is to say more are not already on their way?"

"There is always a risk," Malik argues. "You cannot let the idea that we *might* be attacked rule your life."

"Vampires are not our only concern," I say.

"The witches?" Malik asks.

"By reversing my spell, I have freed the witches from my hex. But they are still at the mercy of their black magic curse. Only now, they have their magic back. If they haven't noticed yet, they soon will."

"And you fear what they might do when they discover their magic has returned."

I nod. "They aren't happy with me."

"They wouldn't dare return here," Malik assures me.

"They aren't of right mind right now, Malik. The evil possessing them is..." I sigh loudly. "They are slowly losing their sanity. Good decisions never come from that mentality."

"You can protect yourself now," Malik says.

"I can, and I will. I owe them nothing."

"And if they come here searching for a fight, are you prepared to wage war?" Malik asks.

I shake my head, causing him to frown.

Because I am not prepared to start a war.

I am prepared to end one.

The blast of energy emitted from my palms slams into Malik. He soars through the air and lands awkwardly on his side. I hear something snap, and he groans as he clutches his side.

I rush over, skidding to my knees when I reach him. I fumble, trying to assess the damage, but he stops me and insists he is okay.

"You did good," Malik says, breathing heavily. "You harnessed enough energy to—"

"Nearly kill you," I interrupt.

I too am breathing heavily. Malik is a ruthless trainer, always keeping me on my toes. He enjoys catching me by surprise, because he insists these little moments are the difference between life and death when we're patrolling. I need to be able to save myself from any attack, and this is the place where I learn how to do that.

I swipe at the sweat that drips into my eyes and try to help him up. He shakes his head, telling me he's fine.

"You need a minute?" I ask.

Again, he shakes his head. I can tell he is keeping something from me. And just when I am about to ask him what, I smell it. *Blood.*

When Malik's gaze reaches my own, I can tell he knows I am aware that he is bleeding. Again, I try to reach for him, and again, he stops me.

"You're bleeding!" I shout, annoyed that he is still trying

to prevent me from assessing the damage done.

"I'm fine," Malik grumbles.

He pushes me away and begins to stand. When he's not paying attention, I steal a glance at his side, peering beneath his tattered shirt before he even realizes I've moved. His skin is charred and black, with a bright red center, as if he was burned by my magic.

"Malik," I whisper, and he catches sight of what steals my attention. "It's bad."

"I'll live. The important thing is you are accessing your magic."

"I didn't even try to . . ." I shake my head, trailing off.

How is this possible? I barely harnessed any energy at all. I sent what I call "baby magic" at Malik—something that was supposed to be an annoyance, not a real threat. I never would have sent a blast of magic at him if I thought I could actually hurt him.

"I think it's safe to say you have not lost your edge," Malik says. "Let's call it a night."

"I hurt you," I whisper.

"Ava, look at me," Malik says, stealing my gaze. "As long as I don't die down here, I don't care what you do. You will never be prepared out there if you hold back in here."

"But—"

"I will be fine. Now leave," Malik says, giving me a clear order.

I walk backward, my gaze stuck on the side Malik is still clutching until the door to our training quarters slams shut before me. He moans, and my heart burns at the realization that I did this. I hurt him this badly. And I didn't even try.

Quickly, I turn on my heels and sprint from the basement.

The moment I enter the kitchen, I find who I am looking for.

Will is gorging on the same food I survived on mere hours ago. Now, the sight makes my stomach churn. I crave blood, and while my body yearns for it, I ache for something else at the moment.

Answers.

"Tell me more about the spell," I say. There is no time for pleasantries.

Will is mid-bite. The fork hovering in the air is carrying a heap of something that smells absolutely disgusting, so I keep my gaze on Will, not the mess of food before him.

"Hello to you too," Will says. He almost sounds annoyed, like he was hoping to indulge in peace.

"Tell. Me. More," I say, emphasizing each word. I cross my arms over my chest.

"Which spell?" Will asks, clearly confused. His lack of answers only infuriates me further.

"The spell you cast to break the curse. Something is . . . off about me."

"Did something happen during training?" Will asks, concerned. He drops his fork and uses the napkin to wipe his mouth. His eyes never leave mine.

I nod. "Something has changed. I think the spell did this."

"Did what?" Will asks, still unsure of what actually happened downstairs.

"It made me . . . *different.*"

"Ava, you *are* different. Just like I am different now too. I already told you this." He breaks my gaze to glance down at his plate. He licks his lips.

I shake my head. "No, you don't understand. I nearly killed Malik during our training, and I certainly didn't intend to do that."

Will sighs and motions for me to sit down, but I don't. I only walk over to him and stand beside him. I don't mean to be so threatening, but I am out of options and in desperate need of answers.

"The ritual required a sacrifice and a power overload. There was only one way to do this. I transferred my power, placing it within you."

As Will explains his part in the spell, he speaks about it so casually, as if he were ordering dinner or making a list of errands to run. He doesn't sound like a man who just gave up his life for someone he has only known for a month or so.

"You . . . You what?" I ask. "How is that even possible?"

"I have always been curious to know if it's possible to . . . *relocate* power. I didn't think I would be able to become human again. I thought that was impossible, but I thought I might be able to give up my powers—so to speak. That was something I researched while looking for a way to save you."

"The coven you found helped you with that too?" I ask.

Will nods. "It's not a common ritual, for a witch to give up their powers, but it is possible. Most witches simply store their magic somewhere with the intention of getting it back one day. Sometimes mothers do this with children, especially if they live around the human population. It was used to prevent exposure. I used it as my only chance at freedom."

"But . . . why?" I ask.

"Because I wanted to be human, and the spell to save you called for a great deal of magic. I had the power you needed, and I didn't want it anymore. It was a simple decision."

"But what does that mean for me?" I ask, still reeling from my training session with Malik.

"That means you have a great deal of magic at your

disposal, Ava, and you need to be careful. Never harness too much. We still don't know what might happen if you do. You weren't meant to carry the magic of two hybrids, but it is now your burden to bear."

My heart nearly skips a beat. I am eternally grateful for Will's sacrifice, because he saved me from death by completing this ritual. But the cost seems too great. I know he wanted to be human, but there might have been another way. Who is to say we couldn't have saved Will *and* me without breaking as many natural laws?

Will must take my hesitation as regret, because he speaks again before I have a chance to respond.

"I don't regret my decision, Ava, so you shouldn't either," Will says, as if he can read my mind. "You needed the strength to defeat the curse, and you got it."

"But by doing this, you have effectively lost your magic. You are mortal now. You must live a mortal life," I say.

Will nods. "I know. I will live and die as a mortal, the way I was always meant to, the way I have always wanted to. You are made for this life, Ava. You want to save the world and live in darkness. I don't. I miss the sunlight. I miss *people*."

"But—"

"My sacrifice was the only way to save you, and you were worth it. You didn't deserve to die by black magic, Ava. You are a good person. You're a good vampire. You fight every day to save people, to help people. You are the kind of person who should live forever."

"And you're not?" I ask.

Will chuckles. "I mean, I'm not rogue-bad, but I'm not quite as selfless as you are."

"And you're sure this is what you want?" I ask, even though

I know this spell must be irreversible.

Will nods. "I am positive. I'm finally happy, Ava. Can't you tell? Can't you see that? I can eat food and watch the sunrise and live a *normal* life. That's all I ever wanted."

"Not in Darkhaven," I say, the words slipping from my lips before I can stop them. I hate myself for even thinking this, even if it is true. Darkhaven is home to too many supernatural creatures. Will will never be safe here—unless he never leaves the manor. And what kind of life is that? I was miserable when forced to stay within these walls. I know Will would never be happy.

Several moments pass in silence between us, and I curse inwardly for saying what I just said.

"Will, I—I didn't mean you can't stay here. I just... I just shouldn't have said that."

I palm my hair, which is still wet and sticky from today's training session.

"You're right," Will admits. "I can't stay here, and I don't plan to."

I suck in a sharp breath. "You're leaving?"

Will nods. "I want to *live*, Ava, and if I stay here, I will spend my days on a vampire's schedule. Besides, I'm no use to you now. I'm weak, fairly useless. I will only be a burden."

"Will," I say as I take a seat beside him. I reach for his hand. He grabs on to my offering, and we stare into each other's eyes. "You could never be a burden."

Will smiles softly. "The way I see it, I've done my part. I cast the spell, made the sacrifice, and now we both benefit. I'm human, and you're stronger than ever. It's time I go home."

"Where is home?" I ask, whispering.

If he isn't going to stay here, then I need to know where

he'll be. Will might not be a hybrid anymore, but I am still devoted to him. Our friendship means more than he'll ever know.

Will shrugs. "Not sure yet."

"Maybe you already are home," I say.

"Maybe. And if I'm meant to be here, I'll come back. I just need some time to figure out who I am now that I'm mortal again."

"Are you scared?" I ask.

Will snorts. "I guess I should be. I mean, I know what lurks in the shadows. I know about the monsters who thrive in the night. And I'm effectively too weak to stop them. But that's how I'm supposed to be. We're meant to be human or witch or vampire. One is always weaker than the other."

I glance away, not wanting to look at him any longer. Never have I felt like more of an abomination than at this very moment.

"Ava, I didn't mean anything by that. I'm not talking about *you*," Will says.

"But I'm a hybrid. I am both witch and vampire, and now I am more powerful than both."

"But *I* was not meant to be that way," Will explains. "I never wanted that life. That's all I'm saying."

"And you think I wanted this life? You think I wanted rogues to attack my coven that night?" I ask, offended. I pull away from him, yanking my hand free of his. His skin is hot, almost scalding.

I miss his cool caress, his confident reassurances. Over the weeks, I came to depend on Will. His visits always held promise of something more. There is a world beyond these walls, beyond the forest of Darkhaven, and Will continuously coming and going meant I might one day escape this place too.

Will shakes his head. "Of course not. No one would wish for such a heinous act. But since then, you have transitioned. You have acclimated. You *thrive* in this world. Ever since that night, you have welcomed the darkness into your soul. You became one with it. You are meant for this world. You want it the way I want the light."

"Does that make me a monster?" I ask.

Will smiles. "We're all monsters in some way, but you are no more a monster than anyone else."

Will and I sit in silence, stealing glances when we think the other isn't looking, and even though he never says it aloud, I know this is the last time I will see him. Tomorrow night, when I wake, he will be gone. He will slip away when the sun is high in the sky, and he will run to the ends of the earth in search of something more.

Will yearns for something that calls to him the way the moon speaks to me. He will run from the shadows, and he will find his recluse the way I have found this manor.

Born from nightmares and powered by darkness, Will has emerged from these muddled depths, and when I look at him, I see nothing but promise. He is a shining example of how wonderful, how life-changing, and how utterly powerful magic can truly be.

EIGHT

First, I feel the heat.

It is blazing, stifling, like fire scorching my skin. Even in my dream, I begin to sweat. The real world affects so much, forcing itself into the astral plane as a stark warning. It is not subtle, and still, I miss all the signs.

I am standing on a beach, basking in the sunlight. This alone should tell me I am not awake, for the sun is never kind to creatures of the night.

The water before me is clear and crystal blue at the same time. It looks refreshing and rejuvenating, like it truly can wash away my worries, my fears. It lies to me, promising to soak my pain, replacing agony with peace. It taunts me with visions of everlasting life. Even though I know this place is a lie, I do not leave. I do not want to be cast back into the darkness that awaits me.

As I walk closer, approaching the water's edge, I notice little fish swimming in the shallows. Every time they try to free themselves by swimming into the murky distant depths, the waves push them back to shore. They continue their pursuit, never giving up even when the odds are so greatly stacked against them. They do not seem to know they will never find freedom. They are forever condemned to live out their lives in this place, knowing the world beyond them is vast and open, but they lack the ability to reach it.

When I dip my toes into the water, these tiny fish swim closer to me, fluttering around my toes before disappearing as I take another step. They are cursed to live within the shallows without the strength or protection needed to survive here. At any point, I may accidentally crush them. Has life always been this cruel? Or am I only noticing it now?

I look down. The water is at my ankles now. It is cool and refreshing, but the heat is still overpowering. It is hard to breathe and even harder to swipe the sweat at my crown. My muscles are weak, stiff.

When I do relieve myself, my hand is coated with my sweat, but I miss some. It dribbles down my cheek. I shiver, feeling every moment it drips down my skin, and I hear the exact second it splashes into the water. The tiny fish swarm that spot, eager to discover the foreign substance that has contaminated their home.

When I look back, glancing over my shoulder, Jasik is there. He stands in the distance, watching me, waiting for my return. He smiles when he notices me watching him. His pale skin—much paler than my naturally bronze skin—is too bright in this light. I shield my eyes against the assault, trying to see him clearly even though the sunlight is blinding.

Jasik says something to me, and I frown. I cannot hear him, and he must know that. I think I ask him to say that again. *What?* I think. But my lips never move. Still, my questions circle in my mind, and Jasik never responds.

What did he say?

Does he need me?

Is he okay?

The sunlight does not seem to bother him. Not here. Not

in this place. On this plane, we are tucked safely in my mind. I protect us from the dangers of the outside world. We can enjoy the sunlight and run barefoot through the night, never fearing what may lie in wait. We are free, safe from the dangers that haunt us at home.

Jasik does not repeat himself. He must be fine, I tell myself. If not, he would have said something; he would have better caught my attention. I think he must be enjoying his time here too, so I look away.

I stare into the distance. The sea seems to be endless, and I wonder if this is the same water that borders Darkhaven. I decide it is not, because that water is dark blue and deep, whereas this water is warm and clear. But if I am not at home, where am I?

I watch the waves in the distance as the water moves effortlessly around my feet. I feel safe here, even if I do not remember how I got here. I do not know where I am or how I found this place, but I feel safe. I want to stay, even if the heat is becoming unbearable.

I am sinking into the sand now, so I begin to move again. I can't stay in one place for too long, because I begin to take root. I want to escape, not feel trapped in yet another prison.

I take another step forward. The water swishes around my heels, and I laugh. I think I hear Jasik say something, but I do not look behind me. Maybe he is laughing too. Maybe he is behind me now, joining me to cool off. The water is at my knees now, but he is taller. He will need to venture deeper, so I do too.

I am wearing a loose dress that flows in the breeze. The bottom hem is damp and clings to my skin as I walk farther away from Jasik. I think I yell for him to join me. The water is cool. I tell him it will help stave off the heat. I hear my voice, but not out loud. I only speak in my mind, and I never hear Jasik's response.

The air becomes heavy with mist, and I let my palms rest against the top of the water. I am so deep now—so deep the water is even colder than before. I close my eyes, listening to the waves, but the world is silent and still. Even the water settles. Everything feels peaceful and pristine. When I open my eyes again, the sunlight shining off the water forces me to squint.

I think I see something in the distance. A dark shadow cruising through the depths. It moves closer, swimming so fast, I can barely keep my gaze on it. My heart is pounding in my chest as I watch its approach, realizing I am too far out. I can never swim back to shore fast enough to escape the creature. I want to call for help, but I know Jasik cannot save me.

When the darkness turns out to be just another wave, it splashes against me, spraying my chest with cool, crisp water. Another wave rolls forward, lifting me so I glide with it. I laugh, and when I settle again, digging my feet into the loose sand, I spin around to show Jasik how much fun it is in the water. He should come out too.

But he is not there.

I am alone.

I stare at the spot where he stood only moments ago, but all I see are embers burning in the ash. Jasik is gone, and the air begins to sizzle.

Next, after I feel the heat, I hear them.

Something crashes in the distance, alerting me to a foreign, unwanted presence. The manor awakens, floors creaking as the intruders enter our domain. The walls whisper as the vampires awaken. The air shifts as bodies sit upright, rising from beds to investigate the commotion.

Jasik shifts; the bed moves. I open my eyes.

No longer am I on the beach, playing in the water. No longer am I free from the burden of life.

I am in the manor, lying beside Jasik. The room is dark, but my vision adjusts quickly. No longer am I plagued with inferior senses. I sit up abruptly, and Jasik rushes to the bedroom door. He turns, facing me, his eyes are alight with fear.

"Someone is here," he warns.

"Maybe it is Holland or Will," I suggest. Both are day-walkers now.

But deep down, I know I am wrong. The sound comes from neither friend. Our enemies are near, attacking during our weakest moment.

Sunlight.

I glance at my bedroom window. The drapes are thick and unyielding. Beyond the shades, the sun is warming Darkhaven, welcoming the living to another blessed day of life.

I am shaking, but I stand and dress quickly. As I pull on my jacket and secure my stake—just in case I am wrong and our attackers really do have fangs—I am buzzing with energy. My skin, my bones, my very core, feels alive with excitement. And I hate myself for it. It has been far too long since I have participated in a hunt, and I am eager to return to normal.

I brush my hair back with my hands, my fingers tangling in my long tresses. I tie a holder, looping it around three times to keep my thick locks in place. I nod to Jasik, letting him know I am ready.

In the seconds it took me to get dressed, Jasik got ready too. He matches me in my attire, wearing dark jeans and a T-shirt. But he has no weapon. After all, this is my room, not his.

I unzip my jacket's inner pocket and toss Jasik my stake. "Here," I whisper.

He catches it midair but frowns when he looks at me. His gaze flutters from me to the stake and back again. I realize he has made the same assumption I have: rogue vampires can't possibly be behind this.

"I can rely on magic. You cannot," I explain.

It is better than nothing.

He nods sharply, as if he understands my silent meaning, and with his hand grasping the doorknob, I take one, final breath.

We emerge into the hallway, the smoky air thick. I breathe in a lungful and hack, leaning against the wall for support. I smelled the fire, felt its heat, but I was not prepared for just how overpowering it would be.

How did we sleep through this?

How did the fire get this bad without anyone noticing?

Jasik grabs hold of my hand, guiding me through the haze. I see nothing but endless streams of thick, smoky air before me, so I rely on my sire, knowing Jasik can walk these halls with his eyes closed and never trip or fall down the stairs—two things I am an expert at accomplishing.

We stop abruptly at a doorway, and I collide with Jasik. My softer frame squishes against his solid body, and I stumble backward, grunting under my breath, offering a vague apology. He does not respond. I am not even sure he noticed I ran into him. Focused on the room before us, Jasik pushes open the door, not bothering to knock. I peer inside with him, watching as Malik dresses. The two brothers say nothing when they look at each other. Jasik turns away and leaves his brother behind.

I catch Malik's eye before Jasik pulls me down the

hallway. For once, he seems scared. If a fire is destroying the manor, the vampires will need to seek shelter elsewhere. But where? Where can they go when the sun is high in the sky? Where can they hide? These questions—and more—are likely looping through Malik's mind too.

We reach Jeremiah's room, again finding him dressing, preparing for battle. Holland is also dressing, his hands shaking as he pulls on a T-shirt. His gaze meets mine, and he tries to smile, but it falls flat, never reaching his eyes. Does he worry for his safety? Or is he also wondering how a house full of vampires are going to survive a daylight fire?

I pull my hand free from Jasik's grasp, and he shouts at me. He fears separation will only lead to our demise, but I can't turn back now. I am already running down the hall, back toward my bedroom. I need to find Will. He is human now, and without a vampire bodyguard, he is doomed.

I reach the door to the guest bedroom—the only room in the manor without a permanent resident—and find it still closed. I knock, hard, hoping I will wake Will before I realize how stupid that is. The manor is *on fire*. There is no time for pleasantries.

"Will!" I shout, hacking as I take in another lungful of smoke. Vampires do not require oxygen as desperately as humans do, and we can hold our breath much longer. If the smoke is affecting me this badly, how are Will and Holland holding up?

I hear someone fumbling behind the door, and when I grab on to the handle, I jerk my arm back, screeching. Grinding my teeth, I seethe, gnawing on my lip until the pain subsides. I glance at my palm. It is bright red, my skin raw, inflamed. As much as I want to run outside and sink my arm into a mound of snow, I do not.

"Will!" I scream again, realizing my friend is in grave danger.

If he is still alive, I think, before I chastise myself for allowing such dark, depraved thoughts to enter my mind. I need to think clearly, stay positive, or we will not survive to see the night.

I stand back, trying to remember the fire safety courses I was taught in school before my mother pulled me out to homeschool me. In this dire situation, I remember nothing— literally *nothing*—from those classes. What am I supposed to do when the doorknob is hot? I remember specific instructions, but I do not remember what they are.

Way to pay attention, Ava.

I make the sudden, and probably rash, decision to kick in the door, praying I can summon magic strong enough to smother the flames before I am engulfed. I know this is Will's only chance at survival.

"Ava, wait! Don't—" Jasik shouts. My sire is rushing toward me, but I have already made my decision. I have to help Will—at any cost.

I snap my leg outward, firmly planting the sole of my boot against the wood door. I thrust forward, kicking it in. The door flies into the room, disappearing into the darkness. The room is silent, still.

There is no fire.

"Will!" I shout again.

"Ava!" he calls from inside the room.

Will responds, his voice muffled. I enter the room, cradling my arm so I do not irritate my wound, but when I glance down, it is gone. The raw, blistered skin is healed. Did I recover? Or did I imagine it all? Was the doorknob even hot? Regardless, I do not have time to consider our circumstances. Not when the manor is soon to be ash.

I run to Will's side just as Jasik reaches the doorway. Will is huddled in the corner, a wet towel wrapped around his face, covering his mouth. His eyes are teary, and he blinks several times as I approach him.

"Come on," I yell, pulling him upright. He leans against me, weaker and lighter than I remember him to be, and we make our way through the smoke. The thick streams of haze seem to be stronger in his bedroom, yet there is no fire. How is that possible?

"What is going on?" Will shouts. He keeps one hand wrapped around my waist and the other covering his mouth, muffling his speech.

Even though I still hear and understand him, I do not respond, because I have no idea what is going on. And I am fairly certain that is not the answer he wants.

"We need to keep moving," I order. We cross the threshold and step into the hallway, where the smoke seems less intrusive. It is still hard to breathe and becoming even harder to see, but there is something about greater numbers that makes me feel safer. Alone in Will's dark bedroom, it felt like all eyes were on me, like we were not alone in the darkness.

The other hunters are cluttered in the hallway, guiding the vampires toward the end, where the stairs will lead us downstairs to the manor's main level.

Then what?

Where can we go?

We can't go outside, and waiting out the fire by hunkering down in the basement seems like an even worse idea.

We are trapped. I see it in the hunters' eyes. No one wants

to admit it, but everyone is thinking the same thought. In unison, we are all aware of our doom, yet everyone fights. We refuse to give up.

"Let's go downstairs," Malik orders, and I nod, breathing heavily.

Will is leaning against me, and a foul odor seeps from him. I try not to breathe it in, but I can't help it. He is too close, the smell too strong. Still, I pretend I do not notice. I think the smell is because of the fire, and I do not want my friend to be even more uncomfortable.

"Where is Amicia?" Jasik shouts.

The others must not notice how badly Will smells, because they pay no attention to him. They do not even ask if he is okay.

"She is safe," Malik responds. "She is leading the others downstairs."

He points down the hall, where the smoke is far too thick to see the beginning of the stairwell. Somewhere in that direction, there are more vampires, there is Amicia, and there are stairs that lead to safety—sort of.

I know we need to get off the second story because the hardwood floors are weakening. I can feel it when I walk. The fire is ravishing the wood, destroying everything this house once was. There was a time it was beautiful, a spectacular sight, but soon it will become ash. The charred remains will be an empty reminder of how vulnerable we are as vampires.

As we approach the stairs, I look into the fearful gazes of a dozen or so vampires. In pairs, they shuffle down the stairs, but I can see the doubt in their eyes. They too are wondering how the hunters can possibly keep them safe. Who will put out the fire? Will and Holland are the only mortals left. Can they do it alone?

All at once, I am reminded of something far more important than *how*.

Why? This is what I must consider, because a better question might be *who started the fire?* And are they still here? What if we are not alone in the manor?

Will's grip is slick in my own, and he grabs on to me more tightly. I pay him no attention as we draw nearer to the vampires.

As we approach the stairs, I see Amicia. She is guiding the vampires to the main level, ushering them into the sitting room below. Beams of light illuminate the first floor as the sun cascades through the many stained-glass windows etched along the manor walls. As long as the fire is extinguished soon, we will be okay. I try to remain hopeful, even when all seems lost.

Will and I take the stairs slowly. I tell him to go ahead of me, but he refuses to release my hand. I agree to stay with him, understanding how terrified he must be. The very night he loses immortality, death comes knocking. Together, we descend, and I watch as he struggles to walk, never releasing my hand, his grip becoming tighter and tighter the closer we get to the manor's main level.

The smoke is just as heavy downstairs as it is upstairs, and while my mind is swirling with questions—like how is it even possible to encounter this much smoke without seeing any flames—my body is screaming for me to run. Every sense within me is alarmed, rapid firing. The hunter within is aroused. She is on edge, prowling in the shadows, certain we are not alone. Something devious, something sinister is among us—and I know I must find it first.

After we shuffle into the sitting room, standing so close that our shoulders touch, everything halts. Time slows as we all begin to realize we have nowhere left to run. We can walk to the kitchen, which leads directly to the basement. We can hide down there, praying the fire does not reach us while also hoping the upper levels of the manor do not fall down, crushing us as we cower in the corners.

We can risk the outside world, running as fast as we can in search of a cave or maybe a vacant house in Darkhaven. We only need sanctuary for the day. Tonight, we can move again. If there was time, Will and Holland could guide us—one by one—through the forest, keeping our skin covered by blankets, praying our sizzling skin does not catch fire.

I know both of these ideas will never work. We are out of options and struggling to maintain hope.

"What are we going to do?" someone shrieks.

Again, we remain silent. Not because we do not want to answer but because we have no answer. There is nothing we can do. I am the only witch with an affinity for water, and I cannot put out flames until the sun sets.

"Ava, can you put out the fire?" Jasik asks, mirroring my inner thoughts. We were separated, and he stands a few feet away from me now. Will is still beside me, hanging on to my arm, gripping me so tightly, I feel nothing else but his hand against mine.

I shake my head, gaze scanning the rooms. I can't put out a fire I cannot find. I fear it might have been started outside, which means I definitely can't get to it. Not until sunset.

"*Where?*" I ask. Jasik frowns, understanding my concern.

The air is heavy with smoke. We can barely breathe, barely see, barely hear over the crackling sound of fire igniting wood.

The heat is excruciating. My skin is slick with sweat, but my mouth is dry from breathing. My tongue is hardening; my lips are cracked. My eyes burn, my lids heavy. My vision blurs, and I try to blink away the tears that fill my eyes. My entire body is reacting to the intense heat wave smothering our home. My skin itches, my hair smells fried, and my feet tingle as the heat worms its way up my legs and settles deep within my cool bones. I fear any moment I might actually combust.

"We can't stay here!" I shout the obvious, knowing there is nothing the others can do.

I blink and squint, noticing a shadow figure looming close behind Jasik. I furrow my brow and stare, desperately and unsuccessfully trying to clear my vision so I can see better.

And then he coughs, and I know that sound. I wipe at my eyes with my one free hand, pulling them back to see my tears have stained my skin, which is coated in ash from the fire and haze.

Directly beside Jasik, I see Will. He holds the damp towel to his mouth, his gaze darting all around him. I can tell he is trying to process what is happening. He no longer has the power of a vampire, but he has the strength of a human. Unlike us, he can walk in sunlight. He can rush out the front door and leave us behind. He can *survive*. But he does not run away. He never leaves our side. His gaze catches my own, and I know he refuses to leave us.

Someone squeezes my hand, and I remember.

I helped Will, I guided him from his bedroom, where the fire seemed to originate. I walked with him down the hall and into this very room. Only seconds ago, he was right beside me, holding on to me as if his life depended on my strength.

But I see him now, across the room, looking as frantic as he did minutes ago.

Someone giggles. Her voice echoes through the room, radiating off my bones. A chill washes over me, and while I welcome its cool caress as reprieve from the heat, I fear the way it lingers.

I am shaking—everywhere. In the corner of my eye, I see her. She holds on to my hand, gripping it tightly. Her fingers slide through my own, linking our bodies together. When I try to speak, I am silenced. My voice mute. My cries are muffled by the smoke.

Jasik stares at me. And then Will. One by one, the vampires turn to face me. Each steps away, clearing a path, encircling me. All at once, they smile. Their eyes narrow, and their Cheshire cat grins tear through skin, exposing teeth sharpened into bloodthirsty points.

I scream, realizing the vampires surrounding me are not my friends. I am alone—again—and terrified I am trapped within a nightmare that has become all too real.

"Did you really think you would get away with it?" she whispers. Her voice is soft but mischievous. Her malevolent presence surrounds me, turning the bright, light-soaked room into a dark, gritty wasteland of death and despair.

As she speaks, the shadows come to life, smothering the light, condemning this time and this place to spend eternity with her—in the depths of hell.

When I finally find the courage to face her, I glance over my shoulder, daring a peek. Her body is gaunt, her bony body nothing but sharp edges and slender limbs. She seems taller than I remember, but I am not surprised. She looks nothing like the woman I once knew.

Her skin is pale, emphasized by the thin black veins that spread like spider webs over every inch of her exposed skin.

The darkness spreads through her flesh, marking it as its own, and when I look at it, it moves, seeping even deeper, claiming control over every part of her soul.

The moment my gaze meets hers, I scream. The whites of her eyes are as dark as obsidian now. Her brown irises are lined with black, and the evil there moves too, blending seamlessly with her pupils. Her eyes have become black pits, hollow and lifeless.

Her breath is rancid and pungent—much like the foul odor I smelled earlier, when my senses were warning me of her presence—and I choke back a gag, swallowing the vomit that spills into my mouth. When she speaks to me, I notice her teeth. They are stained and rotting, black and vile.

She smiles at me and laughs, but she sounds nothing like my grandmother. Because she is no longer *Abuela*. She is a monster, consumed by darkness. I know I should not feel bad for her, but I do. I tell myself she had this coming. This is her fate. She dabbled with the dark arts, danced with the devil, and this is the cost she must bear.

And even though I know all of this—I know she cast that spell as a form of punishment to make me suffer—I still can't help but pity her. Not that long ago, I would have died for her. Now, I want nothing more than to put distance between us.

I rip my hand free, and as I do, I stumble backward, tripping as I tumble to the group. A burst of ash erupts before me, scattering all around, blinding me. I slam against the ground, my hip jutting out to pivot my fall, and pain radiates through my leg.

I blink, the air clearing. Suddenly, I am no longer surrounded by smoke. The haze clears, the looming threat of a fire gone. The formidable odor of flames is smothered, and the world becomes clear again.

I was not dreaming, but I was not present either. While I was trapped in the witches' glamor magic, my world was crumbling. With the spell broken, the illusion shattered, I am sitting on the ground, sinking into a pit of ash. I hold up my hands before me, and they are coated in dust. What I thought was the product of fire was the cremains of my friends. While I was envisioning a world consumed by fire, my friends were fighting for their lives.

I shriek as I scan the room for the hunters. I can think of nothing else until I see them safe. Hikari and Jeremiah are dodging attacks, but Malik and Jasik are nowhere to be found. Where is Holland? And Will? As I search the room, vampires before me combust, and I am forced to watch.

"Stand, Ava," someone says.

Abuela approaches me, not bothering to protect herself from possible attacks. I do not have to ask her why she is as confident as she seems. Surrounding her small, frail frame is a dark aura. The haze seeps into the air around her, coating her skin in a misty black goo.

As the high priestess of her coven, my grandmother has access to the magic and power of every witch beneath her. This evil presence is smart. The dark entity consuming her goodness and her sanity set its sights on her, targeting the most powerful witch in the coven, knowing it will have access to everyone's magic through one elder source.

Immediately, I know what I have to do. I must kill her before she kills me, but that will not stop the evil from spreading. It will simply move to the next in line: my mother.

Born from the witches' actions, this evil will continue to work its way through every member of that coven until it has obtained enough power to leech on to yet another coven and then another. The consequences of using black magic, of dabbling in the dark arts, is so severe that no one should ever be allowed to access it. I can see now that this magic feeds on anger and hatred—and what better coven to provide sustenance than my own? They cast out their own flesh when I became a vampire, and they hated me every second of every day from that point forward. My grandmother was the perfect agent.

I know all of this and more. I know I should move, run, leap from the inevitable attack coming my way, but I can't. I am frozen in time, rooted in place, left only to watch as my own grandmother approaches. Using her air magic to pin me in place, she moves slowly, confidently, with a hideous grin plastered across her face.

While she approaches me, I wonder if I did exactly what the darkness wanted. I reversed the spell, returning the witches' powers so it could feed once again. Slowly, we were dying, but maybe a death at the hands of our own actions would have been better than slowly losing our minds and being eaten alive by whatever this *thing* is.

I think it is fair to say this is no longer a darkness. This evil has become real. It is an entity that craves life and destruction, and I cannot allow it to leave the manor. It must be destroyed, and if it cannot die, then it must be contained.

Suddenly, my grandmother stops. Still several feet away, she raises a single hand before her and summons her magic. The wind shifts, becoming grittier, harsher, and she uses that to solidify it into shards from nothing but the cool, winter breeze. I watch as it swirls round and round, taking form, becoming lifelike in her very palm.

Still pinned in place, my pulse is racing, my heart pounding so loudly, I can hear nothing else. My grandmother drives her arm forward, throwing her magic into the air and aiming her daggers directly at me. I shriek and claw at the floor, desperate to move but unable to go far. I manage to shimmy over, but I am nowhere near far enough away to save myself.

The shards of air poniards slice through the space, and I hear them zipping toward me. They sound like a thousand buzzing bees swarming around my head, but the moment they tear through flesh, something changes. The air feels . . . off.

I blink, and the air magic directed at me is gone, lost somewhere, rooted deeply in flesh, evaporating as though they never existed to begin with. And I feel no pain. Could they have missed me?

I have no time to consider what is happening. The world is spinning, with everything moving too quickly, and I am falling. Something solid slams against me, and I grunt loudly as I fall to the ground. The back of my head smacks against the hardwood floor, and I am dazed. My vision blurs briefly before it clears again.

Something hot and sticky seeps into my T-shirt. It coats my skin as the aroma quickly reaches my nose.

Blood.

The air becomes sweet and thick, my stomach rumbles, and I suck in a sharp breath as I lick my lips. I cannot stop myself from the effects blood has over me. My blood lust is back and stronger than ever before.

I shift, moving upright, and the force that pinned me in place tumbles over. I blink several times, taking in the sight before me, unbelieving of what I see.

Spiritless, he stares up at me. His eyes already glossy, as

though he did not just take his final breath. Blood spews from a gaping wound in his chest. With the air magic disintegrated, no evidence remains except for the hole, displaying flesh never meant to be bared. I see bone and muscle, tissue and blood, but nothing moves, nothing works. Everything just looks *dead*.

He stares up at me, his neck bent back uncomfortably, and his eyes are hollow, empty pits.

And as I stare at Will's lifeless body, now still in my arms, I scream.

NINE

Will is dead. He sacrificed himself to save me from my grandmother's ruthless attack. And now that he lies limp within my arms, I am frozen in place, stunned by what has transpired.

How is this possible? How is he dead?

Only yesterday, only a few hours ago, just before bed, I spoke with Will, and he told me his dreams. He explained why and how he released his magic, choosing to store it within me. He had plans and hopes. He was supposed to live his life before he died a mortal death, not die shortly after setting himself free.

He is supposed to walk out the door, never looking back. I am supposed to break down, crying in Jasik's arms because I have lost yet another friend. But not like this. He was to leave my life by choice, not by my grandmother's hand.

And now he is dead, and I do not understand why. How can things change so harshly and so quickly? Life is not supposed to be this hard, this confusing, this catastrophic. Darkhaven is supposed to be a place where the supernatural finds peace. It should be a safe haven.

I am shaking, and I pull Will's body closer, cradling him in my arms. Tears burn behind my eyes and drip down my cheeks. I speak to him, but he does not respond. I call his name, but he never blinks.

Someone shouts at me. I hear my name. I hear her pained voice as she tries to warn me, but I am broken, frozen in place, unable to move, to think, to react.

I look up in time to see it, to watch it happen, to bear witness to yet another Darkhaven downfall. This time, the cost is too much to bear. My broken soul shatters, and all I can do is watch it happen.

My grandmother is angry, her body practically fuming as she charges forward. Her magic was meant to kill me, not Will. She is furious that he paid the ultimate cost to ensure my survival. I can see it in her eyes. This time, she will not miss.

The darkness radiates from her in staggering waves. Her magic slams into me, pinning me in place. I struggle against it, but with Will's dead weight also slowing me down, I am not fast enough.

Abuela closes the space between us quickly, as if she does not walk but glides forward. She floats over to me, moving so quickly, I can barely keep up with her movements.

The instinctual reaction to push aside Will's body is smothered by my desire to keep him close. I know I can do nothing for him now, but abandoning him like this just feels *wrong*. He would want me to, I know that, but that still does not make leaving him behind in order to save myself any easier.

Again, someone screams my name. I hear her panic, her worry for my safety, but even if I wanted to, I could not safely stand, not with Will's lifeless body weighing me down. I am strong and fast, but my grandmother has proved that she is stronger and faster. The evil residing within aids her, offering my grandmother superior power—even a hybrid is no match for her. I am not stronger than a malevolent high priestess who has access to untapped, raw power, and if I cannot stop her, I fear no one can.

The moment Abuela is only a foot before me, something flashes before my eyes. My rescuer's movements are dark, precise. She moves effortlessly, stopping my grandmother's attack and casting her own devious maneuvers meant to outsmart my grandmother.

My savior is the superior fighter, but I see something heinous in my grandmother's eyes. Abuela expected their protection, their devotion to me. She knew it would come to this.

The moment Amicia reaches my grandmother's side, she slams her fisted hand against the older woman's sternum. Within the palm of her hand, Amicia holds a long, sleek dagger, which is now nestled deep in my grandmother's chest. I hear the moment the blade slices through flesh, piercing Abuela's heart.

My grandmother's eyes nearly bulge from their sockets as she releases a loud cry. Bloody spit bubbles pool around the corners of her mouth as she whispers something into Amicia's ear. The vampire freezes, her body jerking sharply.

I feel the heat radiating off my skin.

I hear the sizzling, crackling sound of flames igniting.

I smell the pungent odor of scorched flesh and burning hair.

I understand what is happening, even if I still am unable to react. Internally, I am connecting the dots, drawing lines to form the explanations my frozen thoughts require. Deep down, I know this will be the stifling heat I need to thaw my body, to force me into action.

And then I see it. I watch it happen. Less than five seconds pass, moments that tick by forever altering the lives of every creature surrounding me.

One second passes.

My grandmother's words reach my ears, and my heightened senses are eager to latch on to them, even though I do not need to eavesdrop to realize what she has done.

Two seconds pass.

Amicia sucks in a sharp, painful breath, an exasperated noise that echoes all around the room. In response to my grandmother's abrupt and unforeseen attack, Amicia lashes out, grabbing Abuela by the throat and sinking her fingers into the frail woman's flesh. Blood spews from gaping wounds, showering the vampire sire in blood.

Three seconds pass.

The other vampires halt their attacks, many losing their lives to the witches in the process. Something flashes behind their eyes, like the quick snap of a trigger releasing. Something—maybe a thought, maybe a feeling—crashes into their minds, and *they know*.

I might have been the only witness up until this point, but no longer am I the only one who knows what has just happened.

Four seconds pass.

Every vampire in the manor save for me falls to the ground. The sharp smack of knees slamming against the hardwood floor sends vibrations through the wood. The sensation tingles, shimmying through my muscles and shaking my innards awake.

By the fifth second, Amicia is lit aflame, and in the very same second, she combusts, bursting into ash and showering down over me. The vampires on the floor scream in agony, as though her death physically pains them as well.

I scan the others until I find him. Jasik is clutching his chest, but he is looking at me. His eyes are burning a bright, neon crimson red. Then he screams, but before he released the heart-wrenching bellow that is preventing me from hearing any other cry, a wave of anguish crosses his face. I see the exact instant it happens. His look of agony punctuates this time and place, marking us in this moment.

Amicia is dead. The reality of her death hits me just as Jasik looks away.

My grandmother falls to the ground, lifeless beside Will. As she exhales her final breath, my mother—mere feet away the entire time her high priestess was attempting to murder me—sucks in a sharp, staggering breath.

In less than five seconds, Amicia died. Abuela died. My mother became the new high priestess of her coven. Abuela's natural abilities are transferring to Mamá—her power, her access to the full coven's magic, and her burdens, like the darkness that consumed her. The evil embodying my grandmother will consume my mother's soul too. And when Mamá looks at me, I know she understands.

I shake, struggling to breathe. The weight of Will's corpse before me and the dusting of Amicia's ash coating my skin is too much to bear. Now, I watch as Jasik falls, physically pained by the death of his sire. Unable to contain the emotions rising in my chest, I allow them to spill from my mouth, and I scream.

As if summoned by my regret, the elements come alive. The air is hot and sticky, causing condensation to drip down my skin, streaking my body with long gashes when it mixes with ash. Outside the manor, the animals react. Birds screech, and I hear the flapping of their wings as they dart into the sky as one massive flock.

The earth moves. The house rumbles, shaking, creaking, jutting from side to side as I release bellow after bellow of hatred and frustration and agony. Pictures hanging on the walls fall to the floor. Windows shatter. Doors slam shut. Books fall from shelves. Furniture topples over. Walls crack.

One by one, the vampires regain their composure, all setting their sights on me, but I refuse to release the earth. One way or another, I will stop the witches from wreaking greater havoc on this town, even if I must sacrifice all of Darkhaven to do it.

"Ava," someone shouts, voice pained.

Jasik is lying on the floor, and he tries to crawl to me. He grips the hardwood with only his fingertips. The scraping sound that follows, as he drags his hands against the grain, desperately trying to pull himself closer to me, is enough to pierce my heart.

My sire, my lover, my savior, is losing this battle. The vampires around him are few in number. All are weakened by Amicia's demise, and they look to me for answers. Already, so many have died. Our numbers have dwindled. One thing is certain. I must save them. Amicia's sacrifice will be meaningful, and I will make her proud.

Grunting, muscles stiff, I tumble over, releasing Will's body from my clutches. He rolls onto the floor, lying beside my grandmother's remains. Now that the darkness has fled, she looks like the woman I once knew, and my heart sinks. It should not have come to this, but she gave us no other choice.

On my hands and knees, I stare at the floor, which splinters. Shards of wood stick up, threatening to end my life if I make just one wrong move. I grab on to one, squeezing it so tightly, I begin to bleed. The stinging pain in my hand overwhelms me, calming my spirit. Slowly, chest heaving, mind spinning, heart pounding in my ears, I attempt to release my hold over the elements.

A hand rests on my arm, jolting me back to this moment, here and now, and I look up at him. Somehow, he managed to reach my side without me ever noticing. I have been so distracted, so consumed by the clutches of magic, I did not even realize that I was in danger.

"Holland," I whisper.

"You did good, Ava," he says softly, smiling. His eyes are pained, his body feels weak. His skin is dirty and stained with blood. "It is time to release the elements now."

Breathing heavily, I nod. I want to tell him that I am trying, but the elements are all around me, surging through the air, empowering me to press on, to release them only when the witches have paid for their crimes. Because they must. They deserve to die. They deserve . . .

That final thought sits with me, sinking in, rooting so deeply it shakes my core. I whimper. What happened to me? What happened to the girl I once was?

Pain.

Destruction.

Death.

These are the only things I have learned from the witches who bore me, who granted me life. Since my transition, I have realized one important fact: my coven lied to me about *everything*. The witches used me to pass down judgment on creatures they knew nothing about. I tried to save them, to help them, to show them the truth, and they cursed me in response.

Time slows as I realize what I must do. Condensation dribbles down my forehead, dripping down the bridge of my nose before splashing onto the hardwood floor. I watch as the droplets of sweat and blood cascade in all directions.

Blinking, I push myself upright, sinking back so that I sit on my heels. My knees burn, my legs ache, and my arms feel numb. My head is throbbing, my heart pulsating so loudly in my chest that I am certain even the witches can hear it.

Still, even as this heat wave makes the air sticky and unbreathable, I am shaking. But not from the cold—from the anticipation of what happens next.

"Mamá," I say. My voice cracks. I sound weak, and I hate that the witches might perceive me that way. Because I am not weak. Not anymore. And no thanks to them.

Holland helps me stand. My limbs feel feeble, and I teeter when Holland releases me. My legs are heavy, and the soles of my feet smack the ground as I walk over to her. Everything feels raw and painful. I am tapping into too much magic, and too much magic is risky.

I wonder if she can see it. I know power is radiating from me in waves—much like the darkness that was seeping from Abuela's pores. But I imagine my power to be bright white, iridescent and shiny. No one will mistake my magic for evil.

Already, the darkness is taking control of my mother. I can see it in her eyes. She is shaking and sweaty. She smells like death and looks weaker than ever before. The evil the witches created is absorbing so much power, it is forming, solidifying, and we all know I can't let that happen. There is no place in this world for such darkness.

"*¿Me vas a matar ahora?*" my mother asks, and I frown.

"Do you truly believe I could kill you?" I ask.

She remains silent, but the truth of my question flashes before her eyes. Yes, she does think I could kill her, but she is coming to that decision based on *her* actions, not mine, because *she* would kill *me*. There is no doubt in my mind that the witches are the absolute embodiment of true evil. It is no wonder they manifested something that would make demons tremble.

"No, Mamá, I will not kill you."

"*Eres débil*," my mother says, spitting the words at me.

"You say I am weak, but it takes true strength to stand before you, after all you have done, and still want peace."

"No peace," she seethes, emphasizing each word. "There will *never* be peace."

Although my mother speaks to me, the sound leaving her lips is not her own. The evil uses her, speaking for her, guiding her to commit its deeds. Her voice is deeper and darker than I ever remember it to be.

I tear my gaze from hers, even though I see the darkness spreading within her, turning the whites of her eyes black. Her skin is wrinkly and pale and etched with tiny black veins. Her hand jerks, her leg twitches, and I know it is only a matter of time before the vile creature she created takes control over her actions. It is becoming too powerful now, and I must stop it—at all costs.

"You are wrong, Mamá," I whisper.

My gaze drops to my mother's neckline, where her talisman dangles from a chain. All my life, my mother has worn the same pendant. Formed by black onyx crystal and wrapped in gold wiring, Mamá once explained to me that it was used for protection. Too bad it did not protect her from herself.

I remember my lessons. Black onyx is the most powerful crystal a witch can use for protection. It absorbs negative influences, acting as a shield to the wearer. Maybe that is why the evil creature focused its influence on my grandmother, who was too stubborn to rely on talismans for aid.

Mamá once said the crystal is wrapped in gold wiring because gold metal represents the sun and harnesses its strength and energy. It is a symbol of power and dominance. Paired with black onyx, this talisman is quite formidable.

The tiny black veins webbing around my mother's frame make a curious pattern around her necklace. They thread everywhere, weaving through flesh to claim her body as its own, but they do not touch the skin surrounding the talisman. The veins make a complete circle, steering clear of the onyx crystal even while consuming the rest of her.

"Peace is the only thing I can offer you," I whisper.

I snatch the talisman from my mother's neck, and the chain snaps. She screeches at the sudden assault, wincing as my fingernails scrape against flesh. I cut her, and she bleeds black ooze. A vile odor seeps into the air, and I swallow down bile. I know I must move quickly, because the evil will understand soon enough.

With the crystal firmly in my hand, I angle it outward and slash it forward. Mamá attempts to deflect my attack, just as I expected her to, but I am much faster than her. I slice the crystal forward, tearing through flesh. Blood pools in her hand, and I clasp our palms together, keeping the talisman at the core. The crystal scrapes against her raw wound, and she grinds her teeth against the pain. Mamá's eyes are full of tears, and they drip steadily down her cheeks. I do not know if she cries out of fear or pain, and either way, I do not care.

"I will offer you the one thing you never gave me, Mamá: *mercy*," I say through gritted teeth.

Mamá shrieks. Her terror is raw and real, her screams

filling the manor. The witches are confused, unsure of what to do. They are loyal to my mother, to this coven, but they are tired. They are weak, and they are afflicted by this curse.

"Repeat what I chant," I order, even though I am confident I can complete this dark curse without the witches' help.

Still, it would be easier if they were on my side. Because of this, I consider adding *if you want to live*, but I decide that is far too dramatic. Either they will aid me or they will not. Either they will live or they will die. I have made my intentions known. For months, I have wanted nothing more than to be on friendly terms, to live in peace. Now is the time they choose.

Life or death.

Peace or war.

The choice is theirs.

I chant the very same words Will repeated the night he transferred his power into me. I use the spell, stealing my mother's magic, knowing her connection to the coven will take their power as well, and I alter the spell so that their magic is stored in the talisman. Black onyx is supposed to be the strongest crystal available for ritual use, and it is time it earns that title.

I have no idea if this spell will work. Mamá is not a willing participant, but then again, neither was I. I had no idea Will was transferring his magic, storing it within me, yet our ritual was successful. If mothers used this spell to keep strong-willed daughters in line, then why can't the tables be turned? Why can't I use it to steal the magic and absorb the evil residing in Mamá, confining it to an eternity within this very talisman?

I continue my chant, ignoring the gnawing realization that bubbles within me. We are not performing this spell within a protected ritual space, but the elements are represented here, and the sun is high in the sky. I have enough power inside of me to overpower this broken coven, and I am determined to make this work.

Mamá begins to shake convulsively. Her grip loosens, so I grab on to her even harder, holding her upright with my free arm. I keep the other clasped around her hand, squeezing tightly so she continues to bleed onto the talisman.

Blood seeps from her palm and splatters onto the floor, but I ignore it. If I have to, I will bleed her completely. In order to contain this evil, I know I must be prepared to sacrifice anyone, including my own mother.

Mamá screams a gut-wrenching howl that ends abruptly, and she falls limp in my arms. Unconscious, she rests against me, and I lower her to the ground.

I hold her hand out before me, and I watch as darkness swirls round and round, being sucked into the talisman. I think I even hear it. The evil this coven created by dabbling in black magic screams in agony, begging for life, for freedom. It sounds scratchy and weak, and I smile, knowing it will be forever contained.

I do not release Mamá's hand until the black veins stamped across her skin dissipate. Only then do I know she is truly free, finally safe. When I lower her hand, I peel back her fingers, taking the talisman with me.

I back away from her, and as I do, the other witches rush to her, collapsing at her side. They do not look at me, but I know they are aware the spell was successful. Their magic, like my mother's, resides in this talisman now, and the witches are cursed to live and die a mortal death. But I like to think that is a far better fate than the alternative.

I glance at Will, who is turning ashy. His eyes are still

open, and they have glossed over. But he no longer stares at me with pain or accusations. The glint in his eyes is gone, but somehow, I know he is at peace. I just wish I still had time to convince him that he did exactly what he set out to do: he found a home; he had a family.

"Are you okay?" Jasik asks, and I crane my neck to look at him, tearing my gaze from Will's cold body.

My sire stands in front of me. He reaches for me, cradling my head between his palms. He still looks broken and pained by the loss of his sire. I sense his exhaustion, his weakness, his hunger. But I also see his love and his devotion to me. That alone will get us through.

I nod and bring my hands up between us, resting them against his chest. He releases my face and steps back, glancing down. I show him what I was holding. Cradled in my palms, I have the black onyx pendant, and somehow, even though I know it is not possible, it looks darker than it used to.

"Their magic is in there?" Jasik asks.

"That is not all," I whisper.

I swallow the lump in my throat, watching as the darkness swirls within the crystal, but it is contained. It loops round and round, moving back and forth, swirling in circles on an endless cycle for all eternity.

"What are you going to do with it?" Jasik asks.

"Keep it," I say, fixated on the swirling magic within the center of the crystal.

"Maybe we should just destroy it?" Jasik suggests, snapping my attention into focus.

I blink several times, clearing my vision. I look up at him and frown. "We can't. That will only release the magic inside. The earth might be able to consume the coven's magic, but it cannot contain the evil inside."

"But if someone gets their hands on that talisman . . . "

I nod, understanding. "He will have control over an entire coven's power, including the dark energy the witches created."

"Then we will protect it," Jasik says.

"We have to," I agree.

"So what happens now?"

I look up at him and smile. I release a long, sharp breath, relaxing as the tension in my shoulders finally loosens.

For months, I have been beaten and abused, bloody and bruised. But now, the war is over. Powerless, the witches are no longer a threat, and while the possibility of rogue vampires will always lurk around every corner, we can live without worry— because eternity is a long time to fret over fruitless feuds.

I glance at the others. Jeremiah and Holland hold each other closely, and I realize true love can survive some fairly brutal moments. It gives me hope, which is something I have not felt in far too long.

Malik and Hikari stand beside them, and the other vampires that survived look to us for guidance. Without Amicia, we will be forced to rebuild the manor as someone else takes leadership, but most importantly, we will find a way to move on, to release the pain and simply *live*—which is all we ever wanted.

Finally, there is peace in Darkhaven.

I glance back at the talisman, watching as it sways from my steady hand. The magic contained swirls relentlessly round and round, ever searching for the stone's weakest points. It yearns for freedom, and I can't say that I blame it. There is something spectacularly awful about being held prisoner within your own shell.

I think about Jasik's question, about what happens next, and I come to one conclusion.

"Now, we rest," I say.

And within the black onyx crystal, the darkness laughs.

ALSO BY DANIELLE ROSE

DARKHAVEN SAGA

Dark Secret

Dark Magic

Dark Promise

Dark Spell

Dark Curse

Dark Shadow

Dark Descent

Dark Power

Dark Reign

Dark Death

PIECES OF ME DUET

Lies We Keep

Truth We Bear

**For a full list of Danielle's other titles,
visit her at DRoseAuthor.com**

ACKNOWLEDGMENTS

Writing a novel is no easy feat. It takes countless people to publish a book—from the writer who drafts the story, to the editor who perfects the words, to the designer who mends the pages, to the marketing team who spreads the message. One person can't do it all, and I am immensely grateful to have such a supportive team behind me.

To Nicki — I dedicated this one to you because, in the short time we've known each other, you've become one of my best friends. Selfless and strong, helpful and understanding, you're everything I strive to be, and you're an excellent role model for Ava, who shares your headstrong personality in all the best ways. I see a little of you in her, and I hope you do too.

To my cohorts, Shawna, Francie, and Heather — It's hard to think of my life without you three in it. Your friendship means more than I can ever explain. Although we're separated by distance, with thousands of miles between us, we're always readily available to lift each other up. That's the kind of friendship that lasts a lifetime.

To my readers and my family — You're the reason I write; you're the reason behind my desire to tell stories people want to read. Writing isn't easy. It's emotionally draining and mentally exhausting, but I can't imagine doing anything else. Without you, I wouldn't be the writer

I am. I love you.

To Waterhouse Press — I probably say this too much, but I am exceptionally proud to write for you. I can't imagine a better home for the worlds I create.

ABOUT DANIELLE ROSE

Dubbed a "triple threat" by readers, Danielle Rose dabbles in many genres, including urban fantasy, suspense, and romance. The *USA Today* bestselling author holds a master of fine arts in creative writing from the University of Southern Maine.

Danielle is a self-professed sufferer of 'philes and an Oxford comma enthusiast. She prefers solitude to crowds, animals to people, four seasons to hellfire, nature to cities, and traveling as often as she breathes.

Visit her at DRoseAuthor.com